Antics & Escapades

A Selection of Adventures

Lost Amongst the Stars
A Parallel Worlds Adventure Excerpt

Fate's Ambition
A James Fisher Thriller Excerpt

Out of the Blue
An Agent Carrie Harris Short Story

Beginning of the End
An 'In The End' Novella

By

G J Stevens

This is a work of fiction. Names, characters, businesses, places, events, locales, and incidents are either the products of the author's imagination or used in a fictitious manner. Any resemblance to actual persons, living or dead, or actual events is purely coincidental.

Copyright © GJ Stevens 2010-24

The moral right of GJ Stevens to be identified as the author of this work has been asserted by him in accordance with the Copyright, Designs, and Patents Act 1998.

All rights reserved.

Copyright under the Berne Convention

British Library Cataloguing-in-Publication Data
A catalogue record for this book is available from the British Library

ISBN: 9798343064377

Lost Amongst the Stars

1

"We'd just come off a three-month run transporting radiated chicken through the Mias disputed zone. You should have seen the size of the gunships we saw almost every day. They were beasts. Each ten times bigger than our rusty hulk and with vacuum blasters covering every surface," Archie said, stroking his thumb and forefinger along the white stubble around his mouth, whilst perched on a mess of white cotton sheets at the end of a hospital bed.

Enraptured heads nodded around the semi-circle of men sitting on the floor, each wearing the same white pyjamas and thin dressing gowns as Archie.

"They'd get so close, causing a blaze of warning lights and alarms throughout the bridge, hoping to hustle us enough to figure out if we were really just transporting food," Archie continued as he leaned forward, making eye contact with each of his audience. "With reports that both sides were as ruthless as each other, it didn't matter to us which side they were on. I'm not afraid to say they gave us the jitters, but that's why MegaFreight paid so well."

Archie cocked an eyebrow as a man's hand shot up whilst he bounced on the floor, a giggle not hiding his excitement.

"Yes, Darren," Archie replied.

"Were you really only transporting food?" the twenty-something teen with greasy, streaked-back hair said with his hand still in the air.

"You're not the star police, are you?" Archie said,

leaning toward the man as he lowered his voice.

Darren burst out laughing and lowered his hand as he covered his mouth and shook his head.

"We might have had a few things stowed away, if you know what I mean," Archie replied, before looking at the rest of the men in turn. "Anyway," he continued. "With a well overdue couple of days off, we landed at the port in orbit around Vorgon, a planet not unlike Earth but long abandoned when an ice age hit, in the Third Nebula of Thairan.

"The port was like Vegas. You could get anything you wanted, and in any shape, size and breed," he added with a wink toward Darren. "All the crew left the ship with our accounts stuffed with credits. After hitting a few bars, before I knew it I'm stumbling about, half off my face. They long ago banned drinking onboard ship, so we were all gasping to let loose."

When a cough sounded from the other side of the room, Archie looked up, peering across the four beds to the only man in the ward not gathered at his feet. Eyeing the scowl from the dumpy guy who looked like a young Danny DeVito, but with jet-black hair across his scalp and around his chin, Archie smiled.

"Anyway, I knew I was on the edge, so I took myself away in search of the other type of action I craved."

Lips smacked around the gathered crowd and the men bobbed forward, a couple rocking.

"So I found a place I'd not been to before, but once you've been to one…" he said, his voice tailing off as he glared back at the man in the bed running his fingers through his thick beard. "You know what I mean. I took a seat and grabbed the menu whilst some stumpy little piece in nothing but a tiny G-string danced in front of me."

"Was she a proper dwarf like Mac?" Darren said with a snort, before his expression fell when he glanced across the beds.

"Yeah, but with more hair," Archie said, beaming over at Mac's reddening face. "She was so short she wouldn't need to get down on her knees, if you know what I mean." The men's eyes widened as at least one of them licked their lips. "But not wanting to spew up what I'd spent so many credits on, I shooed her away and this lime green Andorian bit…" His smile widened as he stopped talking, watching Mac shuffle down the bed whilst drawing up his sleeves.

Each of those gathered followed Archie's smile, but as Darren got to his feet, like a flock of birds the others stood, backing away as the man who rose to half their height came around his bed. He twitched and covered his face with his palms as he stepped back.

"Now, now," Archie said, sneering at the man whose large round belly swayed from side to side as he headed over. "If I call out, you're back in isolation."

"Not today, you focking turd," Mac replied, his voice gruff and low, the words spitting out with venom as he balled his fists, forming the word *hate* across both his knuckles.

"I keep telling you it's fuck, not fock," Archie said, his smile faltering as Mac drew closer.

"Not where I come from," Mac replied, drawing down his brow just as the ward doors burst open.

Archie glanced over Mac's shoulder, but rather than finding a nurse coming to split them up, a tall man with broad shoulders and mousey brown hair stood in jeans and a t-shirt stretching Luke Skywalker's face across his muscled chest. The bottom of a bright red tattoo was just visible below the short sleeve.

"I'm looking for a man," the newcomer boomed, despite being a little out of breath. His perfect white teeth shone out like a lighthouse.

Turning his head to the side, Archie raised his brow.

"I'm looking for a man who has travelled far and wide."

As if not hearing the new voice, and with his cheeks a deep shade of beetroot, Mac continued plodding towards Archie.

"Has anyone here travelled across the Pedrian Gap with their shielding wrecked, but somehow dragged their charge to port whilst having enough energy left to drink everyone else under the table?"

Archie peered back at the new arrival and then down to Mac, who, despite slowing, still advanced, the bands of muscle tight in his neck. The other men stared at Archie, lifting their outstretched fingers towards him.

"Is anyone here a skilled chef that can work with even the foulest ingredient and produce a masterpiece?"

Raising a brow, Mac paused, but not looking around, he took a last step before kicking Archie in the shin. As Archie called out with the pain, Mac turned to Darren, jabbing his finger towards him.

"I'm short, not a dwarf, and if I was, what business is it of yours?" he said, his grumbling voice low.

Darren shook his head, then tripped backwards over his own feet as if the finger had reached across the gap.

"And if you're going to steal my stories," Mac added, turning back to Archie, who rubbed his lower leg in silence, "tell them right. They were impregnated ostriches, you idiot, not chickens."

With a swift prod of his outstretched finger, Mac sent Archie toppling back before spinning around to face the man standing at the door.

"It's just a shame that most people I feed have a moron's palate that couldn't discern the subtleties of flavour if it hit them over the head," Mac said, raising a brow and turning his nose up.

"It's good to see you, Mac," the newcomer replied, his white teeth on show as he beamed with a warm smile.

"Ugh," Mac grunted, his lips curling into a scowl. "I'm glad you're not dead, Travis. What took you so focking long?"

Travis's smile widened, but hearing a sound from the other side of the door, he rushed forward, peering into each corner of the room. Finding no other way out, he picked up a plastic chair and raised it above his head.

"I'm busting you out. Move out of the way." As the chair left his grip, it bounced off the window and rushed back, catching the tall man just below his knee.

"Fock," he called out, hopping on his good leg before twisting around to the opening doors.

"Travis, you idiot," Mac said with a shake of his head.

"Mac, get changed," said a woman whose head appeared between the two doors.

"They're letting me out today," Mac said, glaring at Travis.

"Your cab will be here in five minutes."

2

Travis

"Six months," Mac snarled as the tall double gates at their back swung closed, concealing the orderly already heading away down long the drive, back to the series of low-rise buildings they'd left behind.

Jerking his head back, Travis stopped in his tracks and turned before grabbing Mac's arm.

"Get off," Mac replied, shoving Travis's hand away. Mac had changed into a white t-shirt so large it was as if the staff had not been able to find anything more suitable and had sown together a bedsheet instead. Beneath the top, he wore a baggy pair of black tracksuit bottoms he'd had to roll up to enable him to walk.

Mac swung his foot, catching the side of Travis's ankle with a kid-sized trainer.

"That's how long you left me in there," he spat, then walked off, ignoring the car with the fluffy dice hanging from the rear-view mirror, its engine idling.

"What the…?" Travis called out, rubbing at his leg as he looked between his painful limb and the man tottering away. When Mac didn't look back or show any sign he'd slow, Travis followed, thankful his limp eased with each step.

"Wait up. That can't be right. I got here as quickly as I could," Travis said, a little breathless as he caught up. They were halfway to the entrance and the main road before Mac stopped so abruptly it took Travis by surprise, forcing him to step back in case of a repeated attack.

"It was six months. Are you calling me a liar?" the short man snarled, curling his lip as he glared at Travis.

"I don't know what to say," Travis replied, raising his arms in the air and holding his palms out. "I still don't have a clue what's going on. I can't remember anything past waking up naked in the middle of a field about twelve hours ago."

"Twelve hours?" Mac shouted, narrowing his eyes as he peered up, concentrating on Travis's expression as if looking for a lie.

"Honest," Travis said, but the word sent Mac's eyes tighter. When he took a slow step forward, Travis flinched but didn't back away, instead reaching into his back pocket, the air filling with the kick of vinegar as he unfolded a grease-soaked torn sheet of newspaper.

"After I'd stopped panicking, I stole some clothes strung outside what I think was someone's house, and I convinced the owner of a food place to give me fried potatoes cut into thin strips. I found this staring back when I'd finished."

Travis held out the scrap of newspaper where in the centre photograph a tumble of people blurred in motion with Mac in the middle of the melee, his fist frozen in time as it connected with the chin of a man in a dark uniform.

Mac's brow relaxed, and so did his sneer as he concentrated on the greasy page.

"It says you headbutted a police officer in the genitals because he didn't believe you were a chef on a starship," Travis said, unable to stop himself from grinning. "I'd have known it was you even without the photo. It didn't take me long to find where they'd locked you up. You're somewhat of a local celebrity."

Snatching the page from Travis, Mac tore it to shreds before letting the pieces scatter across the ground. With a grunt, he turned and walked along the road, but at a more reasonable pace. Travis followed.

"What do you remember?" Mac asked after a moment without glancing up, his voice only a little less gruff.

Rather than answering, Travis stared at a white car with blue and yellow stickers along the side and a blue light box on the top as it came into view beyond the gates.

About to repeat the question, Mac held his tongue, spotting the car slowing with two pairs of eyes peering out along the driveway towards them.

"I'm the pilot and co-owner of the Mary May," Travis said when the police car sped up, disappearing behind the tall bushes lining the road on either side of the institution's boundary. His voice was tentative at first, but grew in confidence with each moment Mac hadn't laughed him down. "I guess something sent us from the ship," he said, swallowing hard as he looked around. "And back in time."

Travis watched as Mac's lip curled. After tensing for another attack, he relaxed when the short man shook his head.

"I know it feels like it's the nineteen thirties, although quite different to what we learned in school, but it's two thousand and twenty-four still. I'm certain," Mac said, watching when it was Travis's turn to shake his head. "We haven't gone back in time."

"I don't get it," Travis replied.

"What about the rest of the crew? Do you think the same happened to them? Do you remember anyone else?" Mac said, watching as Travis shook his head. "I can't believe you only lost twelve hours."

"At least you've been warm, and it looks like they fed you," Travis replied, looking him up and down, but regretting the words as Mac's flaring eyes met his. "Sorry. You know what I mean. I understand it must have been hard. I get it. When I came around yesterday, it felt like… I don't know. This place isn't unfamiliar, but I was sure I'd landed a hundred years in the past. Do you know what I mean?"

"It took some getting used to," Mac replied, his voice low as he nodded.

"Do you have any idea what happened to us?" Travis said, coming to a stop. Mac halted, turning around, and Travis breathed a little easier when he saw his expression had relaxed a little. "If it's not a time machine, then what could it be?" he asked, lowering his voice as he leaned closer.

"I don't know," Mac replied, shaking his head. "There are so many gaps," he added, tapping his finger against his temple.

"How much do you remember?" Travis said, turning to the side, but when he got no reply, the corner of his mouth rose. "Um... Out of interest," he said, pausing as if taking time to consider his next words, "do you still remember how to cook?"

Mac narrowed his eyes and glared over.

"I mean, I hope you're still a brilliant chef," Travis rushed to say as he lifted his hands and showed his palms, relaxing when he spotted the twinkle in Mac's eye. Travis softened his voice and leaned a little closer. "Do you remember the Mary May?"

Mac nodded, showing off his stubby white teeth.

"No way," Travis said, his expression lifting. "Do you know where she is?"

Mac nodded again, still with his teeth on show.

"What about the rest of the crew?" Travis asked, his voice tentative.

"I only remembered you when I heard your voice," Mac replied, shaking his head and walking again.

Arriving at the main road, he glanced at the red bus heading towards them.

"What do we do now?" Mac asked, turning to Travis.

"Let's get back to the ship. Maybe the others are waiting for us there," Travis replied, a new brightness in his eyes.

Mac nodded, pushing his hand out into the road.

"Is that a bus?" Travis said, peering along its length before staring at the wheels. "How do we…?" he said, but held back when the bus slowed.

Pulling up the billowing t-shirt, Mac pushed his hand into the pocket of the tracksuit, his pudgy fist clutching a few notes and a handful of change as the bus's air brakes hissed it to a stop.

"It's the money they gave me for the taxi. It should be enough," Mac said and Travis looked down in wonder at the spread of coins.

About to reach out to touch one of the metal discs, he looked up as the doors folded open, then yelped, jumping back when he spotted a straw-coloured Labrador waiting on the other side, the dog panting with its tongue lolling out of its mouth.

Mac tensed, Travis's grip on his shoulders at his back as he used the short man as a shield, whilst the dog led a wrinkled woman down the steps.

With the old lady gone and the bus checked for other animals by Mac, he coaxed Travis past the scattering of filled seats. Travis insisted they sat in the back row to give them a good view of any animals hidden under seats. After a short while, Travis's shakes had calmed, and he'd tuned out Mac's low rumble of laughter, instead staring out at the lush green fields.

Thankful when his nerves had calmed, he noticed a spotty-faced man with bright ginger hair sitting a couple of rows ahead, who kept glancing over his shoulder at them.

With a jab of his elbow into Mac's side, the short cook's laughter subsided as Travis leaned toward him.

"Do you recognise that man?" Travis whispered, whilst Mac glared up at the interruption to his thoughts.

Not relaxing his glare, he followed Travis's nod to the man who, by that time, had turned away.

Mac screwed up his brow as he peered over. When it seemed the ginger guy wouldn't look again, the man lifted his head and glanced over his shoulder, before hurriedly returning when he realised the pair were looking straight at him.

"I don't trust my memory," Mac said. "You?"

"Me either, but was that a glint of recognition I saw?" Travis asked and leaned a little closer, ignoring Mac's low rumbling growl. "What if he's crew and his memory is as bad as ours?"

Mac shook his head, then stood, Travis moving just in time to stop Mac's shoulder from smashing into his cheek.

"What if he's not? Come on. This is our stop."

Travis stood as the bus slowed, following Mac. Uncertain whether to approach the guy, as he passed he glanced down, holding his breath when he spotted the words *Starfighter* across his t-shirt with a spaceship emblazoned on the breast pocket.

3

"It should have been you locked up in that place, not me," Mac shouted over the bus's roaring engine as it pulled away from the kerb.

Without looking back, Travis held his palm up, concentrating instead on Colin, when all it had taken was a whisper in the ginger man's ear for him to step off the bus.

The bus stop sat beside a field of grass stretching out as far as the eye could see, whilst on the other side of the road, the view filled with a sea of tall trees.

"Twenty three," Colin replied to Travis's earlier question. "I'm a mechanic's apprentice for the bus company," he added, with a nod towards the bus as it passed a sign beside the road for *Oglethorpe* and a dilapidated house, which was the only building in sight. "I've been there for six months now."

"Six months," Travis exclaimed, fisting the air as he turned to gauge Mac's reaction. Finding his eyes narrowed and a scowl still wrinkling his forehead, Travis looked back at Colin.

"And your name is familiar," Travis said, his voice booming. "And he's a mechanic," he added, with a glance back down at Mac. "We'd need a mechanic. Wouldn't you think?"

Mac's stare lingered on Travis for a long while, glaring at his wide, toothy smile. When he relaxed his forehead, Travis turned back to Colin and spread his arm around his shoulder.

"Do you remember me?" Travis said, lowering his voice, watching as Colin's brow furrowed before the ginger-haired man shook his head. Tightening his grip on the man's shoulders for a moment, Travis let go and turned to him for a better look. "You're missing memories too," Travis said, narrowing his eyes and leaning closer. "Aren't you?"

The man stared back, taking turns to look them both in the eye before staring at the Jedi Knight stretched across Travis's chest. Pursing his lips, Colin lifted his chin.

"If I was, how would I know?" he said, raising his brow.

"Yes," Travis bellowed, turning to beam at Mac, but found the short man already doddering away, his ample butt swinging from side to side as he shook his head.

Clutching his arm around Colin's shoulders once more, and whistling to mimic the abundant birdsong, Travis led him along a dirt track between the tall trees.

"Don't freak out, but let me fill in some blanks. I hope some of this sounds familiar," Travis said, gripping the man tighter. "We're the crew of a starship, the Mary May," he said, nodding towards the logo on Colin's shirt. "But we're separated from each other and our memories are shot," he added, grinning and flashing his eyebrows at Colin's rapt attention. "I'm the pilot and Mac is the chef," he said, looking over at the man kicking out a surprising pace.

"Where are we going?" Colin asked, as they wound their way along the path beneath the thick green canopy.

"You'll see," Travis replied, but sounding distracted, he let go of the man's shoulders, looking high into the trees when he realised the birds had stopped singing. "Are we near?" he called out.

Mac nodded, then slowed to let them catch up.

"I can't believe I was so close," Travis said to no one in particular as he searched around wide-eyed. Shaking his head, he came alongside the chef, then spotted a vast clearing with light pouring across tree stumps which rose only to Mac's diminutive height. Bright, off-white sawdust and splintered lengths of wood covered the ground, filling the air with its provocative scent.

Halting side by side at the edge of the clearing, Travis marvelled at Mac's lack of a grimace just as a memory rushed into his head of the pair running alongside each other, each of them carrying a stout barrel full of Ivanic rum under their arms, whilst Mac shouted for them to go faster, despite his struggle to keep up.

Closing his eyes, Travis felt as if he could sense the

rest of the crew, but he couldn't find their faces no matter how hard he tried, finding only a deep sense of a connection he knew was forged in the highs and lows of adventure.

The feeling turned to a dread that soon it would be time for Mac to cook, and with an awful smell already forming in his mind, he was thankful when a resounding thump pulled his focus back into the clearing.

Blinking, he watched as Colin fell flat on his back in front of a large rectangular indent in the ground, his eyes closed with a red lump sprouting in the centre of his forehead.

"Idiot," Mac said, scowling at the man laying on his back who neither of them noticed had continued walking into the clearing.

"Huh," Travis replied. "It's like he didn't know she's invisible."

"Sapphire. Reveal the Mary May," Mac snorted.

As the clearing shimmered, Travis held his breath, its intensity increasing like a rising heat haze. Feeling static electricity making his hair stand on end, the area soon darkened, before much of the light went with a blink.

Anyone over the age of three would recognise what resembled the basic form of any flying craft. Cockpit windows waited high at the front of a long, dull silver, unpainted metal fuselage, much like a squashed cylinder with wings on either side. In the middle of each wing and breaking up the sleek lines of each span, stood a large rectangular engine with a yawning, scuffed red opening. Instead of a tail fin at the rear, two smaller engines waited above the main body where scorch marks covered the panels and dents peppered almost every surface. Different coloured sheets of metal clung on in various places with thick, hurried welds that promised their own tales.

On the beaten up panel below the cockpit, a faint row of shapes that were once letters appeared to show the craft's designation.

Keeping the ship raised above the ground were three large stanchions pressing giant metal feet into the soil. One waited under each wing, and another stood under the cockpit where Colin had walked into.

"She's a focking beauty," Travis said, not noticing Mac's raised brow as he stepped around Colin's unmoving body. "I remember falling for her the first time we met."

"She's not a focking person," Mac said, but with no bite to his words as he looked along her lines. "Do you remember how to fly?" he said, his voice a near indistinct murmur. "Focking bitch," he added, almost tripping over the trouser leg that had fallen around his foot as he tried to take a step.

"I'm sure it will come back. Right now I just have to figure out how to get in," Travis said, peering up at what he hoped was a door. After nothing happened when he reached up and rested his hands on the cold metal, he glanced at Mac with a silent question.

"What am I now, your focking butler?" Mac said, standing after rolling up the trousers. But when he didn't bare his teeth, Travis felt a warmth in his chest.

"Sapphire. Open up."

4

As a ramp groaned down below the front wing, Travis gawked, open-mouthed, at the cavernous interior beyond, lit by low lights studding battered metal bulkheads.

With his hand covering his mouth and wide-eyed, Travis took slow steps up the incline, only noticing Mac as he pushed past and into the hold, the short man shuffling across the space before he slipped, his butt slamming on the deck, leaving him sitting upright and stunned in a puddle of liquid beside a dented metal cup.

"Fock," Mac bellowed, then climbed to his feet, kicking and sending the cup clattering across the metal floor, before storming off past what looked like a bundle of clothes further along the wide space, all whilst gripping the low hanging legs of his borrowed tracksuit bottoms to prevent himself going over again.

Mac's call sent a shudder down Travis's spine, leaving him with a dread he couldn't shake until the round man disappeared through the furthest of two doors which slid out of his way.

Alone, Travis peered around the vast space in awe of its extent. Remembering Colin, he headed back outside and, after checking for signs of a pulse at his neck, he dragged the still unconscious man up the ramp by his shoulders.

As the ramp raised behind him before sealing against the hull with a clank reverberating up through his feet, the familiar sound triggered a rush of recollections of the space where he stood.

He remembered caged birds shedding feathers as they squawked nonsense, and gilded boxes encrusted with jewels they were under oath not to open, piled from floor to ceiling. Battered crates filled the vast hall, each tattooed with acronyms and glorious, but indecipherable patterns. Packages of weapons, ore and gems filled his head too, and those were only the ones that stuck out.

Satisfied at what he hoped were memories coming

back, Travis moved towards the only door at the front of the ship. The metal bulkhead swept to the side as he approached, grinding against the floor as it moved. The harsh sound made him step forward, giving it a swift kick.

Alarmed at why he'd felt the need to attack the ship, he stepped through, but his concerns melted away when the door closed behind him with only a light whoosh, leaving him to scan, open-mouthed, across the dim bridge spanning the width of the spacecraft.

After peering across every surface at least twice, he spotted the windows they'd seen from outside were black, but he soon let the thought drift away as his gaze settled on a pair of leather seats behind the bank of controls, each with a joystick and other levers in reach along with a sea of unlit lights, buttons, switches, dials and screens.

In front of the pair of seats and hanging from the low ceiling were a pair of highly polished silver stars each attached to purple ribbons mounted side by side on a square of what looked like cardboard.

Moving his feet just in time, he side-stepped a pile of spilt papers and the half-eaten remains of a compressed food bar he didn't recognise, shedding crumbs on the deck. A pang of hunger tugged at his gut, but reaching the first of the seats, he did his best to ignore the prompt and swallowed hard as his fingers traced the head rest. About to drop into the leather, he spotted a bundle of blue clothes abandoned at the foot of the seat.

Taking the heavy gauge material by the collar, he raised it up, finding a zip running all the way up the front, along with an array of coloured patches across the chest of what he soon realised could only be a flight suit. After folding the bundle, he closed his eyes and sighed as he settled into the seat, marvelling at its familiar hold.

A long moment seemed to pass before he opened his eyes, but as he did, he leaned forward, gripping the joystick and staring out across the confusion of controls.

"You've got no idea, have you?" Mac said from behind as the doors slid closed at his back.

"Not a focking clue," Travis said with a shake of his head.

"Well, that's just perfect," Mac grunted, murmuring under his breath.

Travis glanced over to find the short man leaning down and scowling at the food bar before he corralled the spilt papers into a pile.

"Don't worry," Travis said, jumping from the seat and pushing on a smile. "It'll come back to me," he added, leaning up to the closest set of buttons. But after staring for what seemed like an age, he shook his head, unable to understand the gibberish written on each label.

Despite this, and settling back in the seat, after walking in the world for a day with everything feeling a little alien, he couldn't help but revel in the sense of being home, even though memories were still scarce.

Grinning, he glanced over his shoulder and noticed Mac had changed. Still clearing up the mess into a black fabric bag, Mac wore a fitted leather jacket stressing the round of his belly and wide legged jeans that weren't designed to hug the body so tight. Dark, solid-looking boots capped with gleaming rounds of steel had replaced the white trainers.

"Better?" Travis asked.

"Like you wouldn't believe," Mac replied, raising a brow.

Travis didn't linger, his attention instead moving behind the pilot's seats. He stood and stared past the half-height glass partition separating another four seats mounted on a raised platform, surrounded by a myriad of controls with dark screens lining the walls and set into desks.

Stepping onto the platform, Travis spun the closest seat with his hand, as if by habit, whilst searching for anything that might trigger a memory. When the rush of a motor filled the air, he glanced back to Mac, who gripped the long hose of a vacuum cleaner and ran the head across the deck, grunting with each swing.

"Where did you...?" Travis said, but cut himself off when he spotted something he recognised amongst the panels.

Leaning up to the wall of switches and dials, he scanned across a line of buttons, each labelled with white lines forming different basic shapes. Realising they resembled the controls of a media player, Travis pushed play and his eyes lit up, his smile doubling when every screen came to life.

"What did you touch? Are you a focking moron?" Mac shouted. With the drone of the cleaner fading, he rushed over, shouldering Travis away as he glanced at the glow of each monitor around the bridge. "What did you press?"

Travis reached out to point at the button, but before he could get close, Mac swatted his finger away. Rather than complaining, Travis stared at the digital clock on every screen counting backwards from 47:99:99.

Staring as the digits raced down, Travis tilted his head, wondering what would happen in just under two days. The thought vanished when on the bulkhead beside the closest screen he spotted an envelope taped with three words handwritten in capital letters.

OPEN ME NOW!

Swapping a glance with Mac, who'd also spotted it, Travis stepped up to the bulkhead and gingerly pulled it from the metal. As the paper came away, Mac tutted, licking his finger and rubbing at the sticky mark left behind.

Pulling out a single sheet of paper and avoiding Mac's glare, Travis read aloud.

"DO NOT…" he said, before deciding to finish the rest in his head.

TOUCH ANYTHING.
SAY THIS INSTEAD.
SAPPHIRE. RUN EMERGENCY PROGRAMME DELTA FOUR.

"Um," Travis said, his mouth dry, letting go of the paper as Mac reached up and snatched it from his grasp.

"What have you done?" Mac replied, shaking his head after reading the page then releasing a long sigh. "I guess we should find out how much you've focked up."

Letting his smile drop, Travis swallowed hard.

"Sapphire. Run emergency programme delta four."

5

The already low lights dimmed as a series of strips around the bridge's perimeter glowed blue and a large, disembodied pair of plump lips of the same colour floated midair above the pilot's controls. A rumble of bass rose from unseen speakers.

"I am the Mary May's synthetic autonomous processor for hyper-intelligent reconnaissance and exploration," the low female voice said in time with the moving lips. "You can call me Sapphire. Now bow before your master."

Sharing a look with Mac, Travis swallowed hard.

"I'm kidding, of course," the voice continued in a lighter tone. "Or am I?" she added, lowering again.

The pair swapped another look, but before either of them could speak, the lips moved once more.

"I'm sorry. It's in the script. I was compelled to say it."

Travis's smile returned when, although not recognising the words, he couldn't help but wonder if he might have been behind them. With a glance at Mac, his deepening scowl seemed to confirm his suspicions.

"I am the series four thousand craft AI responsible for the day-to-day operation of Cargo Ship Mary May built by Charon Industries Inc," the voice went on, its tone much more breezy. "I'll give you a minute to take a seat."

Without thinking, Travis sat in the closest chair before swivelling around to Mac and eyeing him with uncertainty, as the short guy scowled at the one next to him. Seeing Travis preparing to stand and offer his hand out, Mac leapt forward.

"Don't you dare," he called, before using the bar meant for resting feet to scramble up.

"The CS Mary May," the voice started again, "is a class four cargo ship and you are amongst the crew."

"How does she know who we are?" Travis said, speaking over her.

Mac shrugged away the question.

"I know this because only the crew's voices can interact with me in my current mode," the female said.

"Sorry. I thought this was a recording," Travis replied, staring at the disembodied lips as they continued to move.

"I am sure you have many other questions, but as

this is a recording, you will have to hope we have thought of everything you might want to know."

Not hiding the confusion on his furrowed brow, Travis relaxed back into the seat.

"I am in hibernation mode and therefore only able to perform basic functions such as providing heat, power, minimal security and door control, and the playback of recordings. Like yourselves, the remainder of the crew scattered across time and whichever planet we are on. They are likely suffering from significant amnesia, amongst other symptoms."

Travis lifted his chin, concentrating on the lips, and was about to open his mouth when he remembered what she'd just said.

"Six Gregorian months ago, whilst working under contract within the Deltoid Sector Union, we retrieved a cargo for a new client. When the client failed to pay the fee on time, we retained the cargo, comprising repossessed equipment from a scientific research facility which went out of business. Amongst the consignment was an experimental quantum nexus travel system."

"A quantum what?" Travis said, frowning as if the words hurt his head.

"From what we know so far, the EQuaNTS was built to travel between dimensions. Based on the fundamental physics you learned in school, there are infinite dimensions, the bounds of which are defined by every decision made by a sentient being. This device bridges the dark matter barrier between them. I'll give you a moment," she said before the lips stopped moving.

"Dimensional travel?" Travis said, swivelling around to Mac, his eyes screwed up.

"It's another focking joke," Mac replied with a disinterested shake of his head. "I bet you a hundred credits you wrote this focking nonsense."

Travis's expression relaxed, and a smile bloomed from the corner of his mouth as he turned back towards the lips.

"This is not a joke," she said, but didn't give them time to react. "For the last five months, the crew of the Mary May have travelled to several parallel worlds."

"Is this for real? It sounds dangerous," Travis asked, looking between Mac and the disembodied lips.

"Whilst conducting compulsory safety inspections on the device as we tried to find a buyer and recover our expenses, a member of the crew inadvertently, and through no fault of their own…"

"Travis," Mac said over the voice.

"…connected the device to the ship's power supply."

"It was definitely you," Mac added, but Travis didn't look around.

"Incompatibilities with this ship's voltage regulation system caused an electrical surge which activated a jump and damaged the machine's interface, forcing the crew to wire it into the Mary May's control system."

"Wait for it," Mac said at Travis's shoulder.

"So far, we have been unable to determine how it is operated, but a simple way to understand what we know is to imagine there are an infinite number of index cards on a Rolodex. The dimension you're experiencing is the current card on display. The next few cards before and after are recent divergences, and would therefore be recognisable to the travelling crew. However, the divergence becomes greater the further away you get from the original.

"Continuing this analogy, to travel to another dimension using the EQuaNTS, you flick through the cards and find the one you want. However, in its damaged state, it is akin to manipulating the Rolodex whilst wearing boxing gloves.

"That, coupled with the creation of a new dimension with each decision made by every sentient being, until we can understand how it works, travel to the same dimension more than once is almost impossible. Likewise, to locate any specific dimensional destination."

Travis's mouth hung open as Sapphire went quiet. Swivelling around to Mac, he watched him glare back with narrowed eyes.

"If it's a joke, it's very specific," Travis said, but turned away as the voice continued.

"So far, we have made five jumps and concluded the human body is not compatible with dimensional travel. The bigger the step away from the starting dimension we take, the more significant the side-effects the crew suffers. These include extreme nausea, lateral and temporal displacement, along with amnesia. As my systems are based around a biological central processing unit, I am not immune to the effects and my safety systems push me into a hibernation state which only a technician from Charon Industries Inc, or the ship's mechanic, can painstakingly pull me out of."

"Colin," Travis said.

"Why the hell did we continue to use it?" Mac said, his voice gruff.

"You're probably asking why we continued to use it after the first time," the voice said. Travis narrowed his eyes. "During the first jump, it became clear that every parallel world is different in some way to the next. Even the smallest of decisions made by an individual can have significant consequences on the world around them. Put simply, the alternatives are not like your home. With a unanimous vote, the crew agreed to attempt to go back to the original point where you would offload the EQuaNTS device before picking up your normal lives again.

"However, we feared that, despite all precautions, the crew could scatter again during a jump. If this circumstance occurred, it is very important that all crew are onboard before you start the EQuaNTS's countdown."

"Countdown?" Travis said with a gulp.

"Here we go," Mac said.

"I will shortly go over the information you will need to gather the remaining missing crew and then to make the next jump. Once the crew is back together and your group's memories have returned, we will process the data collected and adjust the EQuaNTS settings before initiating the forty-eight hour starting sequence. Remember, once started, it cannot be stopped. At zero hour the ship will jump using the loaded coordinates.

"I repeat, it is imperative that you do not press the start button until you are ready, as once started, anyone not on board will be left behind and the chances are infinitesimal that you will ever find the dimension again to retrieve them."

Jumping from his seat, Travis rushed to the playback controls, jabbing the pause button again and again. But no matter how hard he pressed, the countdown continued its retreat.

"Shock and horror," Mac said, underlying his sarcasm with a deep sigh as Travis's head dropped into his hands.

6

"To assist with finding the remaining crew, we have prepared a brief presentation," Sapphire continued, causing Travis to look up from his hands to find a rotating three-dimensional image of a wiry guy in shorts and t-shirt had replaced the floating lips. Black-rimmed glasses accentuated the round of his face, the thick lenses making his eyes seem so large.

"Miles is the ship's navigator. Despite being equipped with intelligence in the top quartile, he has the social skills of a goat. He is always sniffing as if with a perpetual upper respiratory tract infection. Nevertheless, he wears shorts and t-shirts no matter the temperature, or the external weather conditions when planet side. He continually denies that his lack of clothes has anything to do with a constant need to blow his nose. You will probably find him in some academic centre, perhaps a library, or should all other attempts fail, check the local medical facilities for those with hyperthermia."

Travis spun around wide-eyed to look at Mac, pointing at the image.

"I remember him," he said, rushing out the words and watching Mac nod despite what appeared to be some uncertainty.

"Mac is the chef," Sapphire continued, and Travis looked away, filled with a sudden dread as to how the man might react. "He's a neat freak and an angry man. Watch out for his steel toe-capped boots because he likes to take his frustration out on anything at ankle height. You'll find him hunting out ingredients, although it won't make a difference, or in a kitchen brewing up a concoction…"

"What do you mean?" Mac blurted out as the voice

continued. Travis's new grin fell from his lips.

"If you still can't find him in these places, look for Mac either in a bar, jail or a looney bin."

"I'm going to kick your ass," Mac called out, jumping from the seat, but before he could cover the distance between them, Travis raised his feet from the floor, leaving the steel caps clattering into his seat's central pole.

"Sit down. You don't know I wrote it," Travis said, shooing him away. "There's more," he added, as Sapphire spoke whilst the image of a well-built woman rotated in the air.

Wearing black trousers and a black jacket zipped up to her chin, long blonde hair gathered in a tight plait came halfway down her back. Thick muscles bulged against the arms of the jacket, their bulk plain to see despite the size of the image.

"Don't fock with Princess. Ever. Look in gyms or back water bars where she'll have everyone's attention," Sapphire continued.

Pinching his eyes together, Travis nodded.

"Do you remember her?" he said, not looking at Mac. "It doesn't say what her job on the ship is."

Mac only replied with a grunt, the shake of his head reflecting on a dark monitor, but before Travis had time to think, the image changed to himself wearing a figure-hugging military dress uniform.

"What?" Travis exclaimed when Mac let out a long snort of laughter, but when the camera zoomed in on his own confident smile, Travis beamed with pride, mouthing the words as the female voice spoke.

"A military veteran who's distinguished service career was cruelly cut short in its prime by a combat injury, the lead pilot, Travis, is self-sufficient and will be the first to gather the crew. In the unlikely event he is not, you'll find him serving the local community as a fire fighter, or officer of the peace."

"Moron," Mac said, spitting out the word. "You focking wrote this, otherwise she'd have mentioned your stupid ass phobia of dogs!"

"Shut up. She's talking," Travis butted in, holding up his hand when the image changed again.

"Clutch is the ship's engineer, and the only one with a hope of bringing me out of hibernation."

Taken aback when the rotating figure wasn't a balding, middle-aged man, Travis leaned towards the man's dark, dirty skin and a thick dark beard wrapping around the bottom of his face as his stare seemed to follow Travis despite the image's rotation.

"He's perpetually filthy, in part because of his role, and glistens in the light with machine oil. He hates to shower, but somehow, whatever he's caked in keeps things reasonable for those around him. Clutch sleeps with his Universal Tool and you'll find him where machinery gathers."

"I know him," a voice said, cutting in from the doorway. Ignoring Sapphire's continued words, both Mac and Travis turned to find Colin lowering his pointed finger from toward Clutch's image.

Travis drew back, sucking through his teeth when he spotted the golf-ball-sized lump in the centre of Colin's forehead.

"What?" Travis exclaimed as he caught up on what the man had said. Jumping down from the seat, he turned back toward the front when he realised Sapphire had just stopped speaking, but rather than finding a figure floating in mid-air, the disembodied lips had returned.

"That concludes the details of the six crew, and

emergency programme delta four. I look forward to the reunion."

The mouth vanished, and the screen went dark before returning to the countdown.

"Six crew?" Travis asked, twisting around to Mac when he realised what she'd said.

Mac scowled at Colin before turning to Travis.

"What?" Mac replied, easing himself out of the seat, his boots landing on the deck with a heavy thud.

"She said six crew," Travis said, and the chef lifted his chin, squinting in thought whilst holding out his stubby palm.

"You," Mac said, pushing out a finger. "Me," he added as he lifted another digit. "Miles, Princess, Clutch and Colin," he said, before glaring at his raised digits. "Six, you focking idiot. She didn't mention that jumping killed brain cells. Get a grip."

"Of course," Travis replied, nodding as he blinked several times. Then, as he spotted the countdown in the corner of his eye, a rush of energy raced through his core. Doing his best to push the anxiety at the seconds counting down away, he turned to Colin with a widening smile. "Now spill. Where did you see Clutch?"

Continue the adventure by searching 'Lost Amongst the Stars' on Amazon or check out **www.gjstevens.com** for signed copies.

Fate's Ambition

Prologue

I

Fisher followed behind her slender outline, their feet in step along the corridor. His survey swept in time with her dull torch beam as it cut through the darkness, bobbing from the white-washed walls and across the dust of the faded tiled floor.

Agent Harris slowed as they approached a pair of grey, windowless metal doors. In the same moment, both reached around, pulling handguns from their waists.

Fisher caught a distorted reflection, the straight line of his shoulders and the long open cut across his right cheek.

"Did you hear that?" he whispered.

Harris' tight strawberry ponytail bounced as she gave a shallow nod, her eyes pinched in concentration.

Fisher took the lead, pushing the weapon out in front before giving a light touch to the door. The smell hit as it cracked open; not strong, but recognised in an instant.

Without pause he pushed on into the darkened room. From behind, the narrow cone of Harris' torch found a metal table in the centre of the room, soon catching a pasty white ankle laid on top. Fisher watched the light slowly scan up the leg, along a sunken stomach to a faint scar between the curve of shapely breasts and on to the face of a young blonde.

She was beautiful, even in death.

Fisher swallowed as he turned, his heart pounding, looking beyond the light, nodding.

"It's her."

He felt Harris step at his side, the arch of light catching her face, bouncing along its soft angles to the index finger at her lips. In silence they stood rooted to the spot, he strained to hear anything above his breath.

A lifetime passed and Fisher moved his lips to speak, but nothing came.

In an instant, the air pulled from his lungs as he caught a metallic clatter in the distance.

The sound remained still, the pencil beam of the torch searching around the tiled room. He felt Harris' hand, her warmth on his as she pointed up, urging him to look at the ancient ventilation grill in the ceiling.

Pushing the gun into his waistband and stretching out on his toes, his fingertips touched the rough metal as it hung slack against its mounts.

The light faltered and, in the darkness, rusted metal fibres rained down as he felt his way around the edge.

With the light stuttering back, closer this time, he worked the first screw between his thumb and forefinger; the metal sagging more with each painful turn.

The noise came again, at least in his ears, and he crushed the screw harder whilst willing it to speed. Feeling it give, Fisher's eyes followed it to the floor, willing himself to catch the tiny object before it could clatter.

Harris caught it mid-air and he released a breath as the grill, with its decayed surround, fell, smashing to the tiles in a shower of ancient dust.

His hand shot to his mouth, desperate to stifle a cough. With the cloud of dust sparkling in the light, his gaze snapped toward the door.

An eternity passing, he followed the light as it drifted back upwards to the exposed shaft. Feeling a void open in his chest, all hope dashed as the beam lit the rotten, pitted metal rising above their heads.

About to lean close, he stopped when light poured in and he watched as dark figures screamed with rage, bursting through the double doors with machine guns silhouetted, their crosshair dots resting on his chest.

His eyes wide in terror, he stumbled back, only just able to snatch a look to his side. Harris's face resigned, one arm heading above her head, the other lowering the gun to the floor.

"It's over," she said, shaking her head.

"They'll kill us," Fisher replied, watching as the dark figures marched forward, with more piling through the doorway behind.

Staring with disbelief, his heart felt as if it beat out of his chest.

"They'll kill us," he repeated.

Taking a step to his side, he clamped his hand to her wrist and, with all the force he could muster, he blurted out, "They'll kill us."

Her movement stopped.

Harris looked him in the eye, hers as wide as his.

She turned, raising her gun.

A flash lit the room and she fell backwards with each suppressed explosion.

II

Days Later

In the dimly lit corridor, Fisher drew back from the door handle, his tall, smartly-dressed escort getting there first. Instead, Fisher's upturned palm moved to shield his eyes as sunlight surged from the opening reinforced double doors.

"Sorry for the misunderstanding," the suit said, squeezing his lips in a smile.

Fisher smiled back as he walked past, spread his hand out and tipped a shallow bow. As his right leg crossed the boundary, he heard the deep voices bellow from behind.

Chancing a glimpse, he walked as two agents clad from head to foot in black body armour headed the charge through the double doors.

A light breeze blew across his face as a chorus of screams erupted from behind the advancing agent's masks. Without a second thought, Fisher pushed past his escort, ignoring the confusion written across his face and launched himself into the bleak scrubland.

The shouts grew louder as agents poured out and in blind hope he ran towards the chain-link gates. This wasn't the first time he'd been outside of the facility but he was determined to get further than the last time.

A shot rang off, echoing across the landscape as flocks of birds took to the sky. Fisher spun around and wasn't surprised to see eight dark figures gaining with alarming pace, each with an automatic killing machine aimed at his legs.

Pulling up from his flat-out sprint, the agents swarming, he lowered himself to the ground and set the stance he knew he'd be forced to perform.

He placed the side of his head on the soft mossy ground, being careful not to catch the dressing taped to his face and watched with a smile, through the forest of leather boots, the sight of his bemused escort still holding the heavy doors wide.

III

"Mr Fisher, my name is Ross. Brian Ross," the wiry man sitting opposite Fisher announced in a deep English accent, which seemed to contrast to his lean frame. Like the others before him, he couldn't quite place its origin.

Fisher didn't reply. He didn't need to. Brian Ross knew all too well who he was. Instead, after letting thoughts of the fresh air from moments before evaporate, Fisher looked around Interview Room Five with a spark of interest. He'd never been in this particular room before and apart from the numbered door, only one difference told.

It wasn't the dark wooden table or the two plastic chairs he thought were deliberately uncomfortable, or the stale air, he guessed made deliberately cold, or the lack of windows or the single solid wooden door next to his current interrogator. It wasn't that the walls were painted the same cheap magnolia or the harsh fluorescent lights sat in the yellowing suspended ceiling.

It was the long, narrow mirror, or lack of, that he'd spent so many hours staring at while avoiding their questions.

Early on he'd decided the truth was too fantastic, too unreal for anyone to believe, so he'd decided to stay quiet, to ride out the time until they gave up and let him go.

But they had more time than he did.

"The door's locked and I don't have the key," Ross said, stirring him from his thoughts.

Fisher tried his best to ignore the statement but couldn't help turning his head. This was new and he let his expression tell. He tried to let his mind drift, concentrating on Ross's deep-set eyes pronouncing his forehead, drawing out his long, angled face shadowing the surrounding skin.

Fisher smiled as he imagined thick whiskers striking out from his nose.

"It can only be opened from the outside."

Fisher's view snapped back into focus, his gaze following Ross's finger as it pointed to a discrete circle of camera lens in the corner above the doorway.

"Shall we start from the beginning?" Ross said, raising a brow.

Fisher closed his eyes and rubbed his temples.

He'd been in this facility for what he guessed had been four days. During the day he would sit in some drab room where a man in a cliché black suit would ask him questions. Sometimes they would just talk about the weather, football, even though he had no interest; sometimes they would play back his life story, or what their sparse files said.

Sometimes they wanted to discuss the dead girl. So far, he had kept pretty quiet; they hadn't asked about his ability, even though three times now he'd convinced his interrogator to let him walk out of the building. Each time he had been chased down and forced to the floor.

Now they seemed to have figured out how to stop him.

"How's Agent Harris?" Fisher said, repeating the question he'd asked so many times.

"She's fine," Ross replied, giving the same stone-faced response Fisher knew so well.

Still, he didn't believe them.

He'd seen the single bullet smash into her body. He'd watched as she lay contorted, motionless, slumped against the wall with no sign of breath.

His plan wasn't working. For the last two weeks he'd been on a rollercoaster ride, four days at least in this place, and so much happening before. Still, it wasn't time for the ride to end. He knew what they wanted and maybe the only way to get out would be to give it to them, both barrels. But he couldn't be more scared.

Since his parents died, he'd been afraid he'd end up in a room like this, but maybe he had to take the risk. Maybe they weren't going to lock him up, cutting him to shreds to find out why he could do what no one else could.

They'd had a glimpse already; that wouldn't be enough. Was it time to answer their questions? Was it time to tell them why he was in the derelict asylum next to a dead body when they found him? Was it time to tell them how he corrupted Agent Harris so easily? Was it time to tell them why eventually Ross would be so willing to let him go?

What else could he do? They held all the cards.

He was captive. He'd tried his best and he couldn't afford any more time. Fisher didn't know if there was any time left.

He drew a deep breath.

"People just believe me," he blurted out before he lost his nerve.

"Sorry?" replied Ross, raising his eyebrows.

"People just believe me," Fisher repeated, and drew another deep breath as Ross stared back, his face fixed in a frown.

"I don't," Ross said, and a grin grew on Fisher's face.

"You will."

Ross rubbed his teeth against his bottom lip. "They believe anything you say?"

"Anything plausible."

Ross screwed his eyes up, still playing his teeth against his lip.

"Example?"

Fisher looked up at the camera and pictured a room full of black-suited men leaning towards TV monitors.

"If I told you this room was fluorescent green you wouldn't believe me."

Ross nodded.

"But if I told you the corridor was on fire and we need to leave or we'd die, then it would be different."

"Why don't I believe you?"

"It was just an example."

"You can choose if you want me to believe?" Ross said after a pause, his eyes narrowing.

As Fisher nodded, he watched Ross's expression change.

"You'll understand why I'm having a hard time with this."

"Give me your hand," Fisher replied, offering his own rough palm.

Ross looked at Fisher's face, then over his shoulder. After a short pause he lay his left hand down on the table and Fisher placed his palm on top before speaking again.

"Let's say I told you I'm a doctor."

"Not a huge leap," nodded Ross.

"I'm a brain specialist and I trained alongside the best. Smith. Evans. Jones, to name a few."

"Go on."

"I noticed you have a large vein on the right-hand side of your head," said Fisher, pointing to a lump above Ross's temple.

Ross lifted his right hand to the spot. "I've always had that."

Fisher's eyes narrowed. "I noticed it when we first started talking."

"Let's talk about something else, other than me." Ross's tone elevated as he pulled his hand from under Fisher's.

Fisher jerked his hand forward and caught the escaping limb.

"You can trust me," he said, his voice calm and even, lowering his hand back to the tabletop with Ross's hand following. "It's a classic indicator of an issue with blood flow. You need to be careful when you get stressed," he said, then paused again as Ross bit at his lower lip.

"It could cause a blood clot. I've seen it happen so many times before."

Fisher watched as Ross's skin paled with each patiently delivered word.

He leant forward against the table and lowered his tone. "If you don't want a brain clot you should remain calm. Avoid stress." Fisher lifted his gaze towards the door. "I suggest you get some air."

He watched as sweat collected on Ross's hooded brow, his fingers pulling at his tight collar.

"Are you okay? It's getting hot in here, isn't it?"

Ross's eyes widened and his breath laboured. He stood, almost tripping over his own feet as he moved towards the door, his eyes blinking as he pulled, white-knuckled at the handle.

Fisher stood.

"It's locked. Who's going to open it? What if they've forgotten about you? Or popped out for coffee or fallen asleep? What if the camera's stopped working?"

Fisher watched as Ross's eyes snapped wide.

"Let me out," Ross screamed as he hammered on the door.

Fisher moved backward and out of range of the flailing fists. Quicker than he'd expected, a voice boomed from the other side.

"Stand back."

The lock clicked and the door opened. The black metal barrel of an automatic rifle appeared through the gap.

"Down on the floor," screamed the voice.

Without hesitation, Fisher went to his knees, his hands out in front, lowering his torso to the ground. As his head went down to the polished wooden floor, he saw Ross push past the armed suit, gasping for breath, his hands red raw.

Fisher smiled as he turned to the side and settled his head to the floor.

After what seemed like only a few seconds, he heard a new voice, deep and low. A sudden calm came over him.

"Mr Fisher, please take a seat."

Fisher turned his head and saw a silver-haired man, his aged face rough as tree bark, filling Ross's seat.

Lifting himself up, Fisher checked off the uniform in his head. White shirt. Black suit and tie.

The guy was older than all the other agents and wore a smile, reminding Fisher of his long-dead grandfather.

Slowly getting back to his feet Fisher dusted himself with his hands and with deliberate steps, moved back to his chair where he hesitated.

"Please sit down, Mr Fisher," the old guy said, gesturing forward.

Fisher felt like sitting; he felt like listening to this old man's voice.

"I'm Nick Dawson," said the old guy. "That was pretty impressive."

"Thank you," said Fisher, a questioning lilt to his voice as he folded his arms.

Dawson took a sip from a Styrofoam cup. "Do you mind if I call you James?" he said as he rested the cup back to the table.

Fisher shrugged.

"How's the face?"

Fisher pulled his hands up to the rectangle of dressing across his cheek. He'd forgotten about the small injury and nodded across the table.

Dawson's lip curled in a smile. "You've answered at least one of our questions," he said, then paused to take another sip. "But I need you to fill in the rest of the blanks. Please tell me what on earth is going on."

Fisher breathed in the pause. This guy was good. He made him feel safe and Fisher wanted to help. He felt like he wanted to talk. Still, something told him he shouldn't. Something told him nothing would be the same if he gave him everything.

Dawson began to fill the empty space. "We sent Agent Harris to investigate an MI6 operative who'd been acting out of character."

Fisher nodded.

"Harris missed her check-in. You can understand we were alarmed. She's one of our best. We protect our own."

Fisher nodded again.

"It took us a while to find her, and you."

Fisher kept quiet, stifling a smile.

"We knew it unlikely she'd been kidnapped. You probably know by now she's more than capable of looking after herself."

Fisher let the smile bloom.

"So she must have gone by her own free will." The deep lines around Dawson's eyes pushed together as he squinted. "But I'm not sure if I can use the term 'free will' anymore."

Fisher's smile dropped.

"So what's this all about, James?"

"Why'd they shoot her?"

"Self-defence. You'd do the same," Dawson said without pause.

Since Fisher had last saw Harris he'd gone over the moment every time he'd closed his eyes. He knew there was no escaping the reality of what he'd done. It *was* self-defence. It *was* his fault. He'd made her believe their lives were in danger. He *was* sure they were going to shoot, but maybe they weren't after all.

Fisher looked up at Dawson. "How much time have you got?"

Dawson smiled. "As much as you need."

Part One

Two Weeks Earlier

1

"She's gone," Andrew said, his eyes wide as he looked around the group of friends sat at the bench in the darkened garden, bass pouring from the door of the pub at his back.

"What do you mean gone? Gone where?" James Fisher said, stepping towards his best friend.

"She's not there," Andrew said, his palms bared at his front.

"You went in the ladies?" George said, as he moved up to James's side.

"I asked some bird cleaning the toilets. She checked for me. Nothing. I asked if there were any more toilets. There isn't. Had a little scout round, it's still busy, but I couldn't see her anywhere."

With the concern in Andrew's tone, James picked up his phone and called Susie's mobile. He stood, turning with his ear to the air, listening for the ring as he moved, scanning the darkened garden until the speaker replied with the tone of her voicemail.

"It's in her glove box," said George as James hung up. George rose from the bench, leaving the last of the friends, Alan, still sitting clutching his empty glass.

James scowled in his direction. Alan scowled back.

"She's gone off with someone, no doubt," Alan said, tipping the glass to his mouth to catch the last drop.

James's eyes widened. "Suze isn't like that. Don't be a twat and get off your arse."

Alan looked to the dark sky, then, scowling, he stood and followed the others as they headed inside. Separating, they pushed their way through the scores of merry tourists.

George and James were the first to return. As each of them met back outside, they reported finding no sign; between them they'd asked almost everyone but no one could remember seeing her.

"Where the hell is she?" James said, scratching at his forehead.

"I'm stumped," said Andrew.

Alan nodded in agreement at his side.

"She wouldn't go off with anyone," said George. "Would she?"

"No chance," James said, shooting a scornful look at Alan.

"Maybe the drink went to her head when she stood up. Maybe she wandered back to the campsite," said George.

"Possible," James replied. "Someone head back to the site and see if she's there."

"Good idea," said Alan. "We'll go slow and keep an eye out."

Alan and George trooped off through the car park, soon disappearing from view and into the darkness.

Andrew headed back inside while James waited to see if she turned up or if the others reported back. As he paced around the front garden, he stared intently at the people sat at each of the five tables as he drifted back through the last few days.

He remembered the feeling as he woke to the spritely voice of his phone warbling at his ear. Jumping from the bed as if it were on fire, he was ready in seconds, scooping up his heavy pack, smiling when reminded by the weight and swaying to balance as he negotiated the stairs.

That feeling of the night before, his Christmas Eve, the fatigue from a fitful sleep becoming just a memory as he swapped obscenities with Andrew when he found him stood by his own rucksack, tinkering with its contents.

As happened each year, they'd been planning their adventure for over three months. Their close group of friends were this time hiking in Snowdonia; three days of aching legs, dehydrated food and fidgeting for comfort on the hard floor of the tent.

A scream at his back pulled him back from his memories and he span round. It came from a group of friends, still teenagers maybe. A plump girl lay on her back, pulled down by a friend who could barely stand.

James turned as the table billowed with laughter.

He remembered back to the journey; the first hundred miles flying past the windows, lost in conversation. James and Andrew reminiscing, as they often did, about their first meeting in French class where they were forced to sit together at the age of twelve to begrudgingly find they had a surprising amount in common. It hadn't been long before they became inseparable.

Their teenage years sealed the friendship. Passing the test of ups and downs, even when neglect came with the advent of the few girlfriends, and when Andrew's future wife took so much of his time.

They'd settled into adult life together, knew everything about each other. When James left home for university and Andrew started an apprenticeship the opposite end of the country, they still kept in close touch. Sometimes months went by without seeing each other because of the distance, but every time they met it was like they'd only been together the day before.

At university, James made lots of new friends, Susie, George and Alan amongst them, but rather than Andrew feeling left out and drifting away, the friends became mutual. More recently, Andrew had been there for James when his parents had died, both murdered with the case remaining unsolved. Andrew and Susie had brought him back from the brink of doing something stupid.

He owed them his life, even though he didn't think they knew it.

His thoughts turned to Andrew. He'd been back in the pub for what seemed like an age, but checking his watch, it had only been a few minutes.

James turned back to the darkness of the car park.

He remembered Susie had called him on the way up.

"Did you manage to bring your spare sleeping bag?" she'd asked.

"Of course," he'd replied.

"You're an angel, Jim. We'll see you soon. Kisses." He heard her smack her lips together as she hung up.

"Would ya?" Andrew had said, smiling.

"Don't be ridiculous. It would be like doing it with a sister."

"You're an only child," Andrew had said, flashing his eyebrows. "I would."

"Everyone knows you would," James had said, watching the Mondeo slip off the motorway.

James recalled the rest of the journey was taken up with Andrew's favourite subject; grilling James over his lack of love life.

Andrew was often vocal about the subject. The ingredients were there. He knew women were attracted to James. He witnessed it many times. His manual job kept him in shape and gave him a weathered look that women seemed to like.

It wasn't down to lack of opportunity, either; James would be out with Andrew and together they'd flirt with girls, but a rare kiss in a club was as far as it ever went.

As always, the conversation ended with James's hands held up in surrender. He was happy and the time just wasn't right.

Later that morning they'd arrived in the tiny village of Llanberis, their notice only pricked as they caught its brightly-decorated buildings and packs of tourist climbers already congregating on the streets.

James and Andrew were the first of the friends to arrive at the campsite situated under the looming form of Snowdon.

The site was a working farm, formed of small fields no good for crops or animals and instead given over to tents and campfires.

After erecting the tent with practiced ease, it wasn't long before James caught sight of Susie's cream Nissan Micra.

James shook the memory from his mind and looked back to the pub to see Andrew coming through the door, his face falling as he saw him alone.

James's phone vibrated, his heart racing as he fumbled it from his pocket. It was Alan.

"You find her?" he snapped.

"No," came George's voice.

James conveyed the message to Andrew with a shake of his head.

"Shit," Andrew said as he took his turn to scan the faces around the garden.

James was about to speak when George came on the line to interrupt.

"Her car's gone."

2

With heavy feet, James trudged by Andrew's side at the start of the long steep driveway to the campsite. It was the same driveway he'd run to as he'd seen Susie's car approach with those stupid fluffy dice that seemed to obscure her view as they hung from the mirror.

He remembered jogging over, waving his arms as she parked next to the tent before rushing over with her arms wide and squeezing both of them in a long hug.

"Love the new look," Andrew had said, with James watching his eyes widen at the sight of her brown hair now bottle blonde.

"Thanks," she'd replied with her trademark bright-white smile beaming back. "Got a part in a play starting on Monday. Gonna see if I have more fun."

As with George, who had stayed in the car tapping at the screen of his phone, they'd been placed in the same student flat and since the very first party they'd got on like a house on fire.

James and Susie grew very close, partly because during her second year she broke her arm during a violent mugging. The break was so severe she had to have it reset under a general anaesthetic, where she soon discovered she had a rare resistance to sedation and pain medication.

Her condition meant an uncomfortable six weeks of recuperation. James stepped up, supporting her studies, helping her around the house and comforting her as she slowly dealt with the trauma. As the bone in her arm mended, they fused together as friends.

At the end of their time at university, Susie went on to act in many roles. All were minor, either obscure satellite TV or theatre. She was still waiting to hit the big time. With shoulder-length brunette hair, a clear complexion and being neither tall nor short with a slender body, you had to be blind not to find her attractive.

She didn't have a boyfriend the group knew about and she wasn't worried about being single. Andrew would regularly tell James he didn't think her best assets were her contagious smile and her willingness to have fun. Although the guys in the group started off their friendship wanting more, over the last ten years she'd made it clear it was all they were going to get. Susie had become one of the lads. No one needed to moderate their behaviour and there was no need for a separate tent, although James knew the blonde look would be a test for some.

As James saw the dark space where her car had been, he heard Alan's raised voice.

"She's fucked off," Alan said, but before George could reply, James butted in.

"No," James said, panting for breath. "She hasn't," he shouted.

"Where's her car gone then?" Alan said, pointing to the empty space lit only with the moonlight.

"What the hell?" said Andrew, equally out of breath.

"Jump in your car," Alan shouted, but George quickly blocked his path.

"No. We've all been drinking. Anyway, we don't even know where she went."

James shook his head, his breath starting to recover. "Someone must have stolen it. They must have. She wouldn't just up and leave like this."

He looked around his friends and saw their downcast expressions, George's head swaying from side to side.

"Shit," James shouted over and over into the night sky.

"What the hell is she playing at?" Alan said.

James looked up and Alan fell silent.

"Why is a better question," Andrew said.

"I don't believe it," James added, turning on the spot, squinting at all angles, searching for her car in the darkness. "Sure, she can be a little moody sometimes. Can't we all, but I didn't see any sign she was upset. Why the hell would she just up and leave?"

He didn't look up from the dark grass as he pulled out his phone and hit her number. He listened to three rings before the line went silent.

"Susie?" he said, excitement in his voice. A long tone came from the speaker. Wide-eyed, he thumbed her number again and her chirpy recorded voice came back. He turned away and stared up at the blanket of bright stars.

"You okay?" Andrew said, his voice closer than James expected.

"Yeah," he lied, blinking away a vision of her car in a ditch covered in morning dew.

"What about the police?" James said quietly as he eyed the entrance to the campsite.

George's voice came from behind him and James turned to his grey silhouette. "You want to be the one to tell them she's drink driving?"

James didn't reply.

"Maybe someone spiked her drink?" Andrew said as he followed James walking back to the main road. "Then again we'd have seen her leave with someone."

"Drugs wouldn't work," James said quietly as the streetlights of the small village grew brighter as they neared.

"Oh yeah," Andrew replied, his voice trailing off. "We know she's not in the pub."

James looked either side of the thin road, turning away from the brightness of the village and staring along the moonlit road heading out into the darkness. "Then we go this way."

Checking behind him he saw they walked alone with only their footsteps breaking through the silence. His thoughts soon drifted back to the day they'd arrived.

George had eventually pulled himself out of the Micra and strode over to Andrew, feigning a punch to his stomach. As they shadowboxed, James had jumped in, wrestling them both to the ground. Despite being the least fit of the group, George continued to prove himself capable of keeping up with their adventures.

Alan had been the last of the friends to arrive, twenty minutes after Susie and George. As he pulled off the driveway and onto the grass, sweeping his curls of shoulder-length hair away from his freckled face, he parked his Fiesta to the side of Susie's. Moments later, James had herded them towards to the Llanberis trail and the start of their climb.

A smile came to James's face as he remembered the click of the camera-phone whilst they balanced on the snowy peak several hours later. After a quick hot chocolate from the peak's cafe, they made their way down from the sub-zero heat. Heading back through the rock-filled green countryside, passing mountain lakes and ruined stone buildings, he remembered the sense of achievement felt like morphine for their pained calves and blistered feet.

Back at camp they had lifted their heavy rucksacks from their backs and one by one flopped to the floor to bask in silence.

George had been the first to rouse, the pull of the beer in his car too much even for exhaustion to challenge.

He remembered back to university where George had a long beard, smiling as he recalled how George only attended the first week of lectures and spent the next two years blagging his way through the course, going to as few classes as possible.

It had been a miracle it took so long before being kicked out, but leaving university had been the best that could have happened. Almost straight away George got a job and started making something of himself. After a few years working various roles, he got a job in the government doing something to do with roads, getting regular promotions and eventually ending up with some real responsibility.

No one could recall the details of his job; each time George tried to talk about it he read the friend's downcast faces and the subject changed. Last year he got married and a few months ago announced they were having a baby. His wife was due to give birth sometime in the new year and he would become the first of the friends to get into the serious business of having kids.

A long snort of air came from his side and James turned to Alan and chuckled. After finishing the cans of beer, each still warm from the car, they'd light-footed down the drive, floating on thin air without the weight on their backs and wearing comfortable shoes.

They'd stopped at a lonely ATM. Alan pulled out his bank card and James saw the opportunity, but Andrew got there first. As soon as the screen flashed up requesting the amount, Andrew's hand shot out to the buttons and the machine spat out a wad of ten crisp new twenties, to the chorus of howling laughter.

"You bastard," Alan had shouted as he scrambled to grab the notes.

Alan was George's best friend from school and would come over and stay in their halls many times a year. He was welcomed so often into the group, sometimes it became difficult to remember he didn't go to the same university.

Alan had been working his way up the Tesco management pyramid and although he had been assistant manager for a number of stores, he regularly bemoaned the wait to take a captaincy of his own.

Raised by his mum, when she died he'd had no choice but to move to Nottingham with a distant relative.

James felt a deep connection with Alan because of the effort he'd put in to help when James went through his own tragedy. He didn't appreciate it at the time, but Alan knew at least some of what he'd gone through.

"Drinks on you," was all Andrew could get out between panting laughter. The group eventually calmed with a disdainful look from a middle-aged woman waiting to use the machine, not hiding her contempt for the rowdy English tourists on her dark weathered face.

Eventually, as they moved away, Alan found the funny side; it was, after all, a classic trick he'd performed many times before.

Spirits were high and the thirst for lager strong as they headed to a pub just across the road.

It was at that point things had started to go wrong.

3

The Prince of Wales had a small bar to the left of the entrance, occupied by a skinny old lady who looked back at them with disinterest as they came through the door. With their feet sticking to the floor, they peered past the bar to a worn pool table and a broken dartboard propped at an angle on the windowsill.

With the background odour of the toilets on the opposite side of the room, their eyes were drawn to a large TV pouring out the Welsh commentary of a rugby match.

It wasn't what they were used to in London.

Andrew stepped up to the bar and after having to repeat the order three times, he carried pints to a table the furthest from the incomprehensible shouting from the TV. With drinks in hand, the friends recounted the day's tales of adventure and their surroundings faded to insignificance.

Halfway to an empty pint glass, Andrew noticed Susie sitting opposite him had stopped joining in, her arms folded across her chest while staring intently behind him.

"What's up with you?" he asked.

Susie spoke quietly without moving her eyes. "Don't look but there's a guy in the corner who won't stop staring at me."

James and Andrew twisted in their seats to see a young man staring in their direction. His prop forward build and age were the only positive things going for him. With a face covered in acne scarring and a thick white line from a repaired hair-lip, his eyes sat close together and black, unkempt eyebrows seemed to cover the top half of his face.

"I said don't look," Susie snapped. "He's freaking me out," she added, screwing up her eyes and pulling her sleeves over her hands.

George and Alan joined in the stare but still the stranger didn't flinch his look elsewhere.

"You want to swap with me?" James said, tipping his head to the side.

"So he can stare at my arse instead? No thanks," she said, then pushed her hand onto James's forearm. "Sorry. Don't worry, I'll be fine."

The trio changed the subject but Susie wouldn't join in as her eyes continued to flit back to the corner of the room.

"Let's go somewhere else," she said. They all agreed without question and set about downing the remains of their pints.

With the drinks almost empty, James turned to see Susie's eyes widen. Following her gaze, he watched the man swaggering towards them.

"Orright boys and girls?" came his thick North Wales accent.

"We're leaving," Alan announced as he stood.

"Won't you stay for another drink?"

"You're the reason we're leaving," Susie insisted.

"But we haven't had a chance to get to know each other," the stranger replied, pausing to look her up and down. "I really want to get to know you."

Susie pushed past her friends in the direction of the door, but before she got past Alan, a leg the thickness of a tree trunk blocked her way.

"Hey there," erupted James. "Let her pass."

He didn't react. Andrew jumped up from his seat and pushed his hands out but a giant arm shoved him back into his chair with such a force it took the air out of his lungs.

The stranger's gaze never left Susie's face.

James shot a look over to the bar, searching the room for assistance. The barmaid had vanished. Instead, he turned to George and Alan as they sat back down.

It was then James knew they'd already laid their hopes on him. With a sigh, he turned to Susie.

"Why don't you sit back down and we'll have a little chat with our new friend."

She couldn't conceal her concern at his suggestion, but nonetheless she moved back over to her seat.

Showing off his yellow teeth, the guy smiled and sat himself in a spare chair as James downed the last of his pint. Closing his eyes, he drew a deep breath.

"So, my friend, what's your name?" James said as he opened his eyes.

"Gwynn," the guy said, with his gaze still fixed on Susie as she cowered.

"It's nice to meet you, Gwynn." James thrust his hand out to the stranger, but he didn't react.

"Do you know who I am?" James added.

"No. You're not from round here and I haven't seen you on the telly."

"Okay. In that case I'll forgive you."

"Huh," came the startled response as Gwynn moved his attention from Susie for the first time.

"I'm a club promoter from Caernarfon. Just opened a new place in the centre of town. Mention my name on the door and you'll jump the queue."

Gwynn's expression didn't change. "I ain't seen no new clubs. I was in town wiv the lads last night."

"Well it's there."

"Where?" Gwynn asked.

James drew a deep breath. It was all he could come up with. Looking to Andrew and then at Susie, a smile hung limp on his face. Andrew grinned back.

It was easy for them. They thought it was a good way to solve problems. They thought James could just use his party trick and everything would be all right.

The first part was true; he could do it whenever he wanted but the second part was far from it. Something always went wrong and in ways he couldn't predict. It cost him one way or another, some of which he'd have to live with for the rest of his life.

"Right, fuck off you lot," Gwynn's voice boomed. "Me and the lady are going to get to know each other."

Susie turned to James wide-eyed, her hands gripping at the seat.

"James?"

4

"I'll arm wrestle you," James said, and Gwynn's face twisted in what James could only read as shock, but as Gwynn's squinting eyes looked over James's upper body, his mouth curled in the corner and began a deep, slow laugh.

"No problem," Gwynn said slowly as the laughter eased. "If you win you can all go on your way, but when I win," he paused and stretched the fabric of his shirt with his biceps, "she stays." He turned to look back at Susie. "Alone."

Despite avoiding her stare, James knew Susie's eyes were boring a hole in the side of his face.

"No problem," James replied, pushing cheer to his voice.

Susie let go of a whimper as Gwynn rolled up the sleeve on his right arm.

James didn't bother adjusting his clothes; instead, he positioned his elbow on the table, waiting and watching as Gwynn placed his hand in James's open palm.

As Gwynn squeezed, James did his best to ignore the pain, fixing his concentration straight in his heavy-hooded eyes.

"Right, Gwynn, I'm a mean motherfucker. I'm a champion arm wrestler. When I win, which I will, I'm going to crush your hand so you're going to have to get all your love from your left." James twitched the grip on Gwynn's hand and watched as a look of panic shot across his face before Gwynn jumped to his feet, pushing James's hand away as if he couldn't let go fast enough.

"You win, you win."

The friends watched as his bulk disappeared out of the back of the pub.

With Gwynn barely out of the door, Susie jumped out of her chair and rushed for the exit. The guys followed and caught up with her bent double outside the door to a shop opposite, her hands clasped between her legs and breathing rapid. Alan rushed over and she greeted him with a tight embrace; as she squeezed his upper body, she looked at James and mouthed 'Thank you.'

Saying nothing more, they walked along the road, their only aim to get further from that place. Andrew was the first to notice a pub called The Peak Inn.

Set away from the road and behind a spacious car park with wooden benches and parasols in a beer garden at the front, the two-storey building was nestled in a small copse of trees. With stone walls, a slate roof and a large, smart burgundy sign with bold white lettering announcing its name; all set in the shadow of the towering grey Dinorwic slate quarry rising in the distance.

Alan and George headed straight to the bar while the others got comfortable at a bench in the garden. It didn't take long for them to come back with the drinks and a shot of whiskey.

"In one, Susie," Alan ordered as he placed the short glass in front of her. With barely enough time to blink, the empty glass sat upside down in the middle of the table.

"Fucking weirdos," Andrew proclaimed after he chugged down the top quarter of his pint. "Everywhere we go. Dartmoor. The Broads. Snowdon. The locals are fucking weirdos."

"Yeah, it's bloody hot in that bar," Alan replied, putting his fleece back on. Everyone looked at him as he swept his hair out of his eyes.

"No, you lost me," James said, with the rest of the friends smiling in agreement as they waited for the punchline.

"It'll be the furnace in the basement where they get rid of all of the dead bodies," Alan replied.

Everyone but Andrew laughed.

With Gwynn all but forgotten, the conversation turned to work. Alan described his increasing frustration at being passed over for promotion again, with James joking that if he had a supermarket then he would let Alan run it. The others furiously nodded in agreement.

George talked about working in another government department. A sideways move with a slight incline was how he described it.

Andrew told them about being flat-out busy, driving all over the country, but with his job as a medical equipment service engineer, that's all he seemed to do.

Susie talked about her new role in an art house play. It had something to do with murder and incest, set in Scotland. She'd be playing a key supporting role and had been learning her lines for two weeks now. Not for the first time, she told them it would be *the* big one. In turn, they each duly promised to go and see her.

Their gazes then collectively fell on James.

He had excelled at school, college and university and was set for a prestigious placement with Google, but everything changed when both his parents were murdered. James never forgave himself for not saving them from their fate. He never joined the training programme and spent the next few years hidden away from all but his closest friends. Even though Andrew and Susie had dragged him back from the brink, he could never summon the motivation to join the highflying world he'd been told was his destiny.

Instead, James took a job as a tree surgeon. Although intelligent enough to run the company, he preferred to stay as a labourer. It had been five years and the friends made no secret they didn't believe he was content.

His friends patiently waited for his update.

Giving only a shrug of his shoulders in reply, Susie broke the silence.

"We graduated years ago now. When are you going to sort yourself out and get back some of that ambition we used to see?"

"I'm happy," James replied, sipping on his pint.

"You earn minimum wage, you don't use your brain and half the time you're drenched through," Andrew chipped in.

"Yeah, but I go home at night and don't have to think about the job. I work outside and I get to chop down trees."

"He has a point about the trees," added Alan with a wry smile as an unfamiliar silence settled in.

Susie broke in again. "We all know the real reason, don't we? You don't want to get involved with the world. You're going to let life pass you by."

James sighed and looked up to the shadow of the mountain. "I leave it alone and it'll leave me be," he said, clutching at his drink.

"Woah, we're getting a bit deep now," George said as he stood. "Leave the lad alone and get some more beers in."

James turned back to the table and thanked George with a raise of his eyebrows.

Andrew and Alan shared a look, taking the cue and headed to the bar. George following behind.

Susie laid her hands on the wooden bench and stretched across with a sullen expression.

"Sorry," she said. "I shouldn't have said that."

James took her hand in his. "I know what I'm doing."

Susie smiled softly across the table. "But don't you ever think about what could have been?"

James raised his eyebrows. "All the time. That's what keeps me where I am."

Susie stood and walked around the bench. James got up and they wrapped their arms around each other and held on, squeezing tight as George returned from the bar.

"Ah, ain't that sweet," he said. "That deserves a photo," and pulled out his phone. As he pressed the power button, the screen flashed for an instant then went blank.

"Pass me yours," he said, holding his hand out.

James reached in his pocket and chucked over his iPhone while Susie straightened her clothes.

"Get the pub in the background," she said, and pulled James round to the other side of the bench so they were standing in front of the building.

George followed her direction and with a quick call for cheese, the flash blinked and they huddled to see the picture.

"Nice," was all James said, sitting back down.

As if nothing had happened, Susie started suggesting locations in Cornwall for their next adventure, stopping as she noticed a young man striding towards them from the direction of the pub door. In jeans, an Arran jumper and blond quiffed hair, he'd caught her full attention.

Susie looked behind her but already knew there was no one else there. The guy was heading over to talk to her. James had barely seen that look in her eyes before.

"Good evening," the sculpted young man said, smiling to Susie, his accent sounding more like Kensington than Snowdonia. "I saw you earlier. Thought I recognised you. I just had to come over to offer you a drink." He paused as Susie tried to remain composed.

"So what would you like? Sorry, I didn't catch your name," he said, not waiting for her answer.

"Um, Susie," she said finally.

He swapped a phone between his long, thin hands. "My name's Tristan. Would you like to join me inside for a drink?"

Susie shook his hand, but as George coughed, she looked in their direction to see her friends looking back with wide smiles and raised eyebrows. She returned her gaze to the admirer.

"Sorry, I'd love to, but I'm out with my friends."

Tristan tilted his head to the side and shrugged; his smile didn't leave his face as he lifted his hand and a flash burst from his phone.

"A memento," he said as the bright light broke her trance. He turned and walked back towards the door of the pub.

Susie shook her head as she looked back at James. "What a stuck-up twit. But I suppose I'd better get used to that."

Laughter burst out across the bench.

A few minutes later, George reminded them the others hadn't returned from the bar. He was about to go and make sure they weren't grabbing a sly swift one when they appeared empty handed.

"You get thirsty?" shouted George across the garden.

"Some problem with the pumps," said Andrew when they arrived at the table.

"They've taken the order and they'll bring it out," added Alan.

Before Andrew sat down, he reached into his trouser pocket, pulled out two red napkins, dropping them in front of James.

James looked down and then up at Andrew with his eyebrows raised and head tilted to one side.

"Turn them over," Andrew said. James turned the napkins over one by one to see, on each, what looked like mobile phone numbers. Two names, Clare and Fay, were scribbled above in Andrew's handwriting.

"You're married," James replied.

"They're not for me, you ejit," Andrew said, smiling.

James pushed the napkins to the centre of the table.

Andrew snapped them up and shoved them back in his pocket. "Waste not, want not." He then turned his attention to a short barmaid dressed in the black and white uniform of bar staff across the country as she carried a tray of drinks, heading in their direction. Andrew reached for his wallet.

"It's already been taken care of," the barmaid said in an Australian accent.

"Was it a Toff in a cream jumper?" asked James.

She burst out laughing.

"He owns the place," she said and turned around, still chuckling as she went back through the door.

"Looks like you made an impression," George said to Susie.

The banter continued, with subject again turning to where they'd set next year's adventure. After settling on canoeing along the River Wye and after finishing the free drinks, yawns spread around the table. They soon decided to call it a night. Dragging themselves up the steep driveway, they returned to the quiet campsite and were soon sound asleep.

James woke with an insistent but gentle pressure tugging at his arm. Struggling to rouse, his head felt stuffed with cotton wool as nausea rippled upwards from his belly. Thankful to the darkness, he eventually peeled open his eyelids.

"Did you hear that?" Susie said in a whisper, her breath at his ear.

As his brain deciphered her words, James strained to hear, but could only make out the rhythmic breath of his friends and a gentle breeze through the trees. He ached for sleep.

"What did you hear?" he croaked as he pushed his voice to speak.

"Footsteps outside the tent," she whispered, an edge of fear in her voice.

"It'll be someone going for a wee."

"And they were playing with the zip."

James couldn't miss the concern in her voice and despite his muscles screaming to relax, he dragged himself onto his front. Still inside the sleeping bag, he felt for the zipper of the inner doorway. With his vision slowly adjusting, he found the thin metal tag and pulled it up enough to squint out through the open flap.

Losing the fight with his heavy eyelids and barely able to take in the darkness of the porch, a wave of nausea stopped him before he could take in the first sight.

James closed his eyes and felt for the zip to draw the canvas back into place. Turning back, he faced Susie with his eyes still shut.

"It's fine. Must have been a dream. Come here," he whispered as he put his arm out.

Without protest, Susie lifted her head and his arm went under. Feeling her body envelop him in a warm glow, the tension bled from his muscles. As the first ebbs of unconsciousness lapped, he heard the outer zipper move just as sleep overwhelmed him.

***

James woke to a cacophony of birdsong, a shrill assault to his ears as a flock welcomed the new sun. With his head still clouded, his vision blurred to the bright morning.

He had no idea of the time but from the spluttering and snoring of his friends he guessed it was still early. Searching for his phone he realised his arm was still around Susie and eased himself from under her, thinking it best to save any confusion or comments from the others.

Moving, he felt the urgency to pee and pulled himself from the sleeping bag, attempting and failing to open the first zipper quietly.

Once through the porch, James watched the low sun chasing away the morning mist from the quiet campsite and, turning to his left, he congratulated himself on the choice of pitch.

Ignoring the stiffness in his legs, he jogged the few paces to a copse of trees.

With his urge relieved, he shook his groggy head and wandered through the dew-laden grass.

His attention caught on debris scattered around their tent. At first, he thought rubbish had blown across from other pitches; then he recognised his backpack and saw his clothes spilt out in a pile.

Alan surged from the tent and sprang to the copse, holding his stomach. His retching startled the birds from the trees.

"What the fuck happened here?" said Alan, appearing from the tree line, his face pallid and squinting as he wiped his mouth with the back of his hand.

"Susie heard something in the night. She woke me, but shit, I thought she was dreaming."

Susie emerged from the tent and scanned the scene with surprise. George and Andrew followed bleary-eyed.

"Is anything missing?" she said.

"My stuff seems all there, but it's soaking wet from dew," said James as he sealed his pack.

"Mine's okay," Alan came back as he picked up a couple of t-shirts by his feet and stuffed them back in his bag.

Andrew and George nodded as they picked up their untouched packs.

"Looks like yours took a direct hit," Andrew said, looking at Susie whilst he pointed to her small camping sack sitting empty on top of its former contents.

She rushed over to her bag and poured through the pile. James headed over to help but she shook her head as he neared.

Her lips pursed and her brow furrowed as she scooped up the contents, shaking off the dew. James crouched next to her.

"I'm sorry, Suze. I should have gone out and checked." He looked to the others dotted around the tent. "Shall we call the police?" he said, and watched as Alan shook his head.

"It was probably just kids," he said, colour returning to his face.

"Or drunks," George added, turning to look around the site.

"I must have disturbed them when I unzipped the inner door," James said.

"Anything missing?" asked Andrew as he came over and rubbed Susie's shoulder.

"Don't think so," she said with a solemn look down to her pile of belongings.

"Police won't do shit then," Alan replied.

George stood. "There's no harm done. Let's just get it tidied up, have some breakfast and get on with our day."

They soon each agreed they didn't fancy wasting their time waiting for the police when nothing had been stolen.

With the mess cleared, the friends gathered around Andrew's stove and drank welcome hot tea.

James turned to Alan, noticing his skin had paled again.

"How much did we drink last night?" he said, shaking his head.

"Five or six pints?" Susie replied, furrowing her brow as she tried to remember.

"Well it's bloody strong up here," Alan said before running off into the copse.

"Probably the altitude," Andrew said with a chuckle. "Feel a bit poor myself."

Topping up their liquid breakfast with cereal bars and after a quick change into fresh clothes for Susie, they packed up the gear for the hike, locking the rest of their belongings into the cars.

With the rest of the site stirring, they set off past the farmhouse and into the western side of the national park.

The day turned out as they'd planned and before they knew it the friends saw the camp ahead on the new horizon. Each agreed it had been a thoroughly enjoyable day, but with sore feet and legs they were ready for food and the evening's entertainment.

After confirming the tents and the cars hadn't been abused, they renewed their strength with hot pasta and once again headed down the steep driveway to find the car park of The Peak Inn full of brightly-coloured VW camper vans, four by fours and estate cars, the insides stacked past the windows with bedding, bags and outdoor gear.

Each of the garden benches were full, so together they piled through the door where the humidity and heat had intensified from the day before. The Peak Inn seemed to be a tourist favourite.

With the others heading back outside to wait for an empty table, James and Alan squeezed through the throng of revellers and joined the long queue for the bar.

After a short wait listening to a rabble of accents, none they recognised as native, and with a tray full of drinks, they joined their friends who stood on the edge of the car park. Huddled together, they watched a steady stream of new arrivals, while keeping a watchful eye on the prized benches.

After half an hour and with fresh drinks, none of the bench's occupants had made any sign of moving.

George paid particular attention to an older man sat alone reading a newspaper at a bench a few metres away.

Susie sipped her drink. "Let's go to the shop, buy some beers and take them back to the tent."

Alan nodded, rubbing his calves.

"My legs are killing me. We need to do something," he said.

Andrew shook his head. "Nah, there's much nicer scenery here," he said with a grin turned in James's direction.

George nodded towards the middle-aged man he'd been watching. "That guy hasn't drunk a single drop since we got here," he said.

Alan's eyes widened. "Why don't you do your 'spooky' on him? Get him to piss off," he said.

James glared in his direction. Then, looking to each in the group, he watched them smiling back doe-eyed. When he got to Susie, he watched as she rubbed the length of her legs. Andrew raised his eyebrows and beamed an exaggerated smile.

"Yeah, come on. It's not like they're losing a customer, is it? The old git hasn't touched his drink in hours."

"You have to admit he'd be much more comfortable in that crap hole down the road," piped in George.

"For God's sake," James snapped and handed his pint to Andrew.

The friends watched as he walked over to the occupied bench and spoke a few words. They almost let up a cheer as the guy picked up his drink, gulped down the remains and stood up, heading away a little unsteady across the car park.

James sat down, looked at his friends with open hands and lifted his eyebrows.

"Nice one," said Andrew, as he sat down and placed James's beer in front of him. "So what did you say?"

"I just asked him politely if he was going to be long. He said he was just about to leave." James waved his hand out in front of him. "And I didn't need any special powers."

George laughed but Andrew and Alan stayed silent.

"Would have been funny if you said there was free booze in the Prince, or the landlord would be out in a minute to kick him out."

"Or your wife's at home being shagged senseless by your best mate," Alan said, butting in whilst laughing.

Susie shot him a dirty look.

James sighed. "No, it wouldn't."

"Why?" Andrew said, shaking his head.

"There are always consequences," James said to the four blank expressions staring his way. "It took me years to understand."

He sat in silence, but their looks urged him to explain. "When I make people believe, they have no reason to doubt. If I told him there was free beer in the other pub, then he's going to think they're giving away free booze, right?"

Each nodded.

"So he goes to the boozer, orders a beer and expects it to be free. I don't know this guy, I don't know how he's going to react to finding out he has to pay. He knows for sure they were giving it away for free, so maybe he thinks the barmaid's lying, doesn't want to give him the free beer. He gets into an argument and he's kicked out, maybe even barred or gets into a fight."

George was the only one still nodding.

"Let's say I tell him his wife is having an affair. Arriving at home he finds her sitting on the sofa or in bed, but no best friend. He wholeheartedly believes me, so he accuses her and maybe, best case scenario, they split up because he doesn't trust her anymore. Worst case scenario, he goes to his best mate's house and tops him."

As James finished his sentence, he formed a gun with his hand and fired it at Alan's head.

"I'd be responsible for that. I would have killed him." He paused and stood up. "If I had to say something then I would have said that his wife misses him and would be grateful for some company. My way, what's the worst that could happen? She may actually be missing him and I've just put a little love into a tired relationship. If she's not missing him, who's going to get upset with their other half going home early to spend some time together?"

James got up from the table and headed into the pub.

When he came back from the bathroom the subject had changed, with George trying to tell a story about work, but Andrew soon changed the conversation.

A few minutes later, as Andrew told Alan about a new car he was looking to buy, with Susie and James only half listening, Andrew jumped up from the bench with his phone ringing in his pocket. As he wandered off into the car park, George and Alan headed off to the bar.

Susie looked behind her and then checked across to Andrew. When she saw he was out of earshot, she leant across the bench toward James.

"I wanted to talk to you about something. While we're alone, I mean."

James leant forward, squinting as she moved closer.

"What is it?"

"I met this guy. Well, I've been seeing this guy, right," she said, causing James to tilt his head to the side as she fumbled for her words. "Not for a long time," she paused and pushed straggles of blonde hair behind her ears. "Well," she paused again and pushed at hairs that weren't there, "a couple of days ago, in the morning, he, uh, asked me to take part in an experiment."

"What sort of experiment?" James asked, leaning closer still, a playful smile rising.

"A social experiment, with, um," she pushed more stray hair behind her ears, "you guys."

James's eyes narrowed and the smile slipped as Susie rubbed the back of her neck.

"I said no," she quickly added. "But..." She stopped talking as she caught sight of Andrew bounding back over.

"Just wifey checking up on me. What you guys conspiring about?"

"Oh, nothing." Susie turned back to James and mouthed 'later' as Andrew's attention went back to his phone.

In quick succession, George and Alan were back with drinks and the night continued.

After a couple more rounds they started to think about calling it a night.

"I'm just going for a piss," said George, as he rose unsteady on his feet.

Susie stood at the same time. "Me, too," she said, and they both disappeared into the pub.

A few minutes later, George returned lifting his jumper over his head.

"It's still a flipping furnace in there," he said as he sat back down. "Must be a busy night in the basement."

James raised a smile as Andrew lifted his hands above his head to stretch.

"It's actually all right here. Probably because everyone's a tourist," he said.

James looked at his watch. "Shall we piss off when Susie's back? Long drive in the morning."

Looking around, he saw his friends nodding with empty glasses in front of each of them.

James looked at his watch again. "She's been a while."

"Probably all this crap we've been eating," said Andrew, rubbing his stomach through his fleece. "I'm going for a piss."

Five minutes later, Andrew returned with narrowed eyes and looking like he was searching for a lost memory.

5

James was first to wake. Despite having barely slept, he bolted upright as last night's images flashed through his mind like the pages of a flip book. He'd walked with Andrew in the dark for what seemed like hundreds of miles, arriving back at the tent at the first signs of light to find the others fast asleep.

Scanning around the tent, a spark of hope hinted it had all been a dream, but his shoulders soon sank with Andrew in the space where she'd slept the night before and his spare sleeping bag lightly scented with her perfume pushed to a pile at his feet.

A dull ache grew in the pit of his stomach with the building regret he hadn't done more last night.

James raked open the inner tent and scrambled to the outer door. Jabbing his feet into his hiking boots, he pulled the flap open, his breath catching at the sight of the field empty of her car. He scanned the grey skyline;

mist hung close to the ground, hiding the great mountain they'd climbed the day before.

Bundling back into the tent, he jabbed at Andrew's shoulder. "Get up, we're going to find her."

Andrew's eyes opened, his stare blank and sleep wary before the memory hit.

Together they stood around shallow tyre tracks in the mud where her car had been.

"She got stuck," George said, stretching out a yawn.

Alan rubbed his eyes as he joined them. "Makes sense. She was pissed, gave the pedal abuse," he said.

James turned and walked away; George followed behind.

"I had a thought," George said, calling softly after him. "Why would they be cleaning the toilets at that time of night?"

James stopped and turned. "Someone made a mess I guess."

He turned away, pulling out his phone, listening to her voicemail as he walked. This time he left a message.

"It's James. I don't know what's going on and I don't care. Just call me. Call someone. Call anyone and let them know you're okay. Please." He clicked off the call and flicked to the number for Susie's flat in London. It rang until eventually her flatmate's recorded voice came on the line. He didn't leave a message.

George and Alan jumped in the Fiesta and James joined Andrew in the Mondeo. They'd agreed to each search twenty miles out, Alan east and Andrew west.

Andrew prodded the trip timer and at the bottom of the driveway they headed right towards Capel Curig. Within a minute they were outside of the limits of the tiny village and after another ten had covered five miles of sparse road, dotted with the occasional row of isolated houses, their silent heads sweeping side to side.

At ten miles, a short row of houses on the left and a shabby petrol station on the right broke up the craggy landscape; the weathered antique pumps rusted with names of oil companies long forgotten. A paint-peeling sign hung on a tall wooden workshop, displaying a faded list of services.

About to move out of sight, James saw a beige Micra parked at the rear in his peripheral vision.

"Turn around," he blurted, slamming his hand on the dashboard. "Susie's car."

He kept his head pivoted towards the shed as Andrew sped up before wheeling the car around at a break in the stone wall.

"You're kidding?" exclaimed Andrew as they pulled alongside one of the pumps.

In front of them sat a Nissan Micra with its nose in the green workshop and its rear sticking out to the tarmac. The bonnet stood raised at an angle, but there was no one around working on it.

Only taking his eyes from the car for a split-second, James tapped at Alan's number.

"What's her reg number?" James shouted.

"It's a 56 and it ends L E G, pretty memorable," came George's voice from the phone's loudspeaker.

James hung up and let out a deep breath. It wasn't her car.

He turned to Andrew and they pulled back to the road, winding their way between the dry-stone walls. It wasn't long before the dial clicked over to twenty-two miles.

Andrew slowed and sluggishly turned the car at a deserted crossroads.

Arriving back at the campsite James tried to swallow down his dismay at seeing George and Alan already had the tent flattened.

They climbed out, Andrew meandering in their direction while James stayed back with the phone in Susie's flat ringing in his ear.

"Susie?" James said, excitement in his voice as he recognised her words.

"No, Kate." Susie's flatmate.

"Hi, Kate, it's James," he said, his voice flattened.

"Hiya," she said. "Everything all right?"

He instantly knew Susie wasn't there. "Yeah, not bad," he said, unsure of what to say.

"What's happened?"

"Um," he paused and drew a deep breath. "Susie's driven off and I wanted to see if she'd gone home."

"Oh," she said, not sounding too concerned. "Do you know why?"

"No."

"You know how she can be sometimes," Kate said back.

James frowned. "No."

"Look, she's probably just... I don't know, hooked up with someone."

"She's not like that."

There was a pause on the line.

"No, she's not," Kate's voice came back, quieter than before. "Look, I'll let you know if I hear from her. And you let me know, too."

James nodded as he said goodbye. He called Susie's mobile, listening as it went straight to answerphone then looked up at all that remained of their weekend; a rectangle of flattened grass.

As the group set off walking back down the drive, the village appeared drab and worn in the flat grey light, like Vegas in the daytime. Without the brilliance of the sun, even the colourfully-painted shops failed to brighten the street. The cafe sat empty and the village centre bare, save from a grey-haired old lady shuffling, her back bent at an extraordinary angle, wheeling a tartan shopping trolley across closed shop fronts.

Stepping into the bright red cafe, its windows steamed, the four turned towards The Peak Inn opposite and a flurry of glass smashed as a lone cleaner emptied large black bins at the side of the pub.

They sat by the windows, James watching as the others exchanged concerned looks.

"Stay or go?" James said, putting words to everyone's question.

"Go," said Alan immediately. "There's nothing we can do here. She'll turn up at her house or at some friends. Could even have gone to Cardiff. All the while we're hanging around here getting old."

"I think I agree with Alan," added Andrew, not moving his eyes from the menu. "The more time goes on, the more pissed off I'm getting."

"She's fucked this weekend completely," Alan chipped in, shuffling in his seat.

James knew they were all looking at him, waiting for his reaction as he stared in the direction of the pub. He left them waiting until the teenage waitress broke the silence to ask for their order. When James stayed quiet, Andrew ordered for him.

Out of the corner of his eye, he saw Alan prodding Andrew in the ribs.

"Mate?" Andrew said, looking towards James.

James turned in his seat and met Andrew's widening eyes.

"What happens if she's lying in some ditch somewhere? We've all seen these roads. It could be weeks before she's found," James said.

"We've looked. Let's take it slow on the way out, use the route she would have taken home," Andrew replied, his voice unusually soft.

Silence fell again until the same waitress brought plates piled high with fried food with his friends setting upon them like wild beasts as he turned back to the pub.

James's stomach churned as he looked down at his own carnivore's feast and ran his fingers through his short hair. Rotating his phone in his left hand, he prodded the food with a fork in his right.

He wanted to be close to her, close to where they'd last seen her. He wanted to stay until he knew she was safe.

Pushing the plate away, he saw George look up from his meal, his eyes bright with an idea.

"Why don't we take advice from the professionals?"

James tilted his head to the side, raising his eyebrows, a pang of hope shooting through his chest at George's words.

"Let's see what the police say?"

The group swapped glances, nodding in turn with full mouths.

James sat staring whilst George headed outside to make the call, coming back within a minute.

"Someone's going to call me back."

"What now?" said Alan.

They ordered more coffee.

George's phone rang within a couple of minutes and he rushed back out the door.

Five minutes later, he sat back down at the table. James tried to read his expression.

"Spoke to the duty Sergeant in CID and there's nothing official they can do. He's going to check the national computer and see if her name has been logged, or if there were any Jane Doe's reported along the route to her home address. The procedure should be to check with the hospitals but there are at least forty between here and London, so he said it would be best just to let him check." He paused, looking around the group before turning to James. "I'm not sure it was helpful or not," he paused again, and James gave a slight nod, "but he said people go missing all the time. Most of them are found within a day or two. He's going to call me if he gets any news."

"What did he say *we* should do?" asked Alan as he drained his mug.

George threw him a look before he turned back to James.

"There isn't much we can do, other than to check with friends."

"So we go home, yeah?" Alan nodded with enthusiasm.

"I guess so," replied George, looking at James's blank expression.

"Then what?" James said, speaking for the first time.

"If we don't hear anything within twenty-four hours, we need to call the police and report her as a missing person."

Everyone's eyes were on James. He cast his gaze to the table and slowly nodded.

"We should tell her parents," George said.

James slunk back in his chair and rubbed his temples. "Maybe she's there. I'll do it," he replied, his voice low as he stood from the table and headed out the door.

As he walked to the car, he tried to summon the words. He rang Kate and could hear her concern. He didn't need to ask; he knew Suzie still hadn't turned up.

With her parents' number in the phone, he took a deep breath and made the call, relieved when her dad answered.

"Hello, Mr Whitmarsh, it's James. Susie's friend from university."

"Oh. Hello, James." James heard the surprise in his voice. "Aren't you away with Susie?"

For a second time his question didn't need to be asked. "Yes, we were, Mr Whitmarsh, but Susie left early."

"Oh, okay," the deep voice replied, leaving James hanging in silence for a moment. "Was everything all right?"

James took a deep breath. "She didn't tell us she was going," he paused as he chose the words. "And she drove off in the middle of the night."

"I see," was all Mr Whitmarsh said before James relayed all of what they had done so far and the advice the police had given. "I can see what Susie sees in you."

They agreed to keep in touch and said goodbye.

James stood in the street, replaying the conversation over in his head, the last phrase catching in his mind; I can see what Susie sees in you.

He turned back to the cafe and saw his friends walking towards him. At the cars, James told them how the call had gone and saw tension relax from their faces.

"I'm staying," he said.

"Don't be silly," Andrew said, patting him on the back. "Get in the car."

James looked around the street, his gaze stopping on The Peak Inn nestled at the bottom of the grey background. He turned to Andrew, holding open the passenger door with George already in the back seat. Alan smacked him on the back and jumped in his car, speeding off barely before the door shut.

James took a deep breath and walked up to the car door held open by Andrew but couldn't help feeling he was making the wrong decision.

***

Her eyes opened to pitch black, the throb at her temples easing as she sealed them back shut. She'd have to get up for painkillers soon, but for now the comfort of her bed still held her tight.

She could feel the makeup smeared to her face and knew her mum would be pissed.

More washing, she could almost hear her say at the sight of her pillow shadowed in black and brown. *You'll learn when you have a family of your own.* Just one phrase she was tired of hearing. But she'd get away with it today. Her mum wouldn't stay upset for long; after all, it was her only daughter's eighteenth birthday.

Tomorrow would be another thing. Tomorrow her mum would have her world ripped apart. Tomorrow she'd tell her mum that she'd been offered a place at the Academy of Art in San Francisco.

It was easy to predict how upset she'd get.
Your heart condition? Your medicine?

She'd tell her mum the scholarship included medical insurance which covered her condition and all the drugs. There was even talk of taking part in a trial; a chance she'd not have to take those foul-tasting pills every day for the rest of her life.

Her mum would still get angry because they hadn't talked it through.

She'd tell her mum she would come home every Christmas and some of the summer. It was, after all, only a three-year course.

Her mum would say she wanted her near to keep her safe.

It would be fine, she would reply; there was as much chance of trouble in America as there was in their sleepy backwater.

The throb had grown and it was time for water and pills. She didn't remember drinking that much last night but when the girls got together anything could happen.

Her body felt heavy as she sat up; a memory flittered back from the recovery ward. She swung her legs around, stubbing the heel of her foot on the cold floor a couple of inches below the mattress. Her hand dropped over the edge of the bed.

Why was her mattress on the floor?

Distracted by her pain she struggled up, swinging herself in two attempts, rocking on her backside; the pounding pain in her head sending the question of the missing carpet quickly away.

She walked with stiff legs in the pitch black in the direction of her door, arms outstretched, feeling for the texture of her flower-papered walls.

Sooner than expected, her fingers stubbed against a surface much rougher than she remembered.

Pain clouded her head and her hand brushed her bare leg. She touched her top, realising she wore the short outfit from last night.

Her chest throbbed. She knew the procedure and stopped moving, her hand instinctively reaching to the faint scar over her faulty muscle.

"Deep, slow breaths. Deep, slow breaths," she said out loud, her voice low and hoarse.

Dragging herself along the wall, guided by her hand across the rough surface, her throat rasped for water and head pinched with pain. Her hand caught familiar sharp contours and she felt herself relax with the realisation she was at her friend Pippa's, at least by the feel of the square light switch.

She closed her eyes as her head still pounded with each furious beat. Her fingers pushed the long switch.

The light seared through her eyelids before she could flash her arm across her face.

She stood and waited for the wave of pain to subside, concentrating on the drum in her chest. She slowly moved her arm and, squinting hard, opened one eye for less than a second before it jammed closed.

As her brain caught up with the patterns in the brightness, she knew something was wrong.

Curiosity and fear triumphed over the pain and she opened both her eyes to a slit. She pushed her temples in an attempt to null the agony of light coursing to the back of her eye, but when her focus fixed, her hands dropped to her side as she took in the alien view.

The boarded-up window.

The yellow-stained mattress.

The lonely bucket in the corner.

"Where the fuck am I?" she screamed.

Unpick the rest of the mystery by searching 'Fate's Ambition' on Amazon or check out **www.gjstevens.com** for signed copies.

Out of the Blue

1

Gasping for air, everything was suddenly so bright. I coughed, another following, and then again until it felt as if the fit would never stop.

As I eventually calmed, I couldn't bear to open my eyes. The world around me was too hot and dry. My limbs ached even before I tried to move, and it felt like I was stuck to the ground whilst being baked from underneath.

My head seemed bulbous and too heavy, not able to lift. As I struggled, making no progress at all, whatever I lay on shifted with each movement.

After listening to the lapping waves for what felt like such a long time, I opened my eyes, then squeezed them closed against the brightness. When eventually I'd built up enough courage, I lifted my arm, squinting and only just able to shield my face from the high sun.

Swallowing, as if for the first time, my throat felt like sandpaper.

When the pain relented just enough, I saw a beach with a foamy sea beyond.

Turning my head with such care, I watched the pristine bleached sand which seemed to go on forever, finding myself alone except for the odd drift of varnished wood and scattering of frayed carbon fibre.

Twisting to look to my left, I hoped for some feature, a house perhaps, but my head only made it halfway before a sickness clawed up from my stomach.

After a breath to aid the pounding in my head, I looked along my body whilst trying not to strain.

I wore a bright orange vest, a life jacket, but limp and tight against my skin.

My legs were bare other than the covering of sand. My toes naked, red and pointing to the sky.

Voices came from my left, and I tried turning again, but my vision went black with a thought flooding through my mind.

Who the hell am I?

2

With another gasp dragging air into my lungs, the light seemed less bright behind my eyelids. When the noise of my breath echoed back, I forced my eyes open.

If I'd had the strength to move, I'd have flinched at the sight of four beautiful faces peering down.

Realising there was a hand on my shoulder, that of a woman with long blonde hair, she pulled away. Another woman stood by her side, a brunette, just as beautiful, her eyes wide with relief.

The others were men, both as handsome as each other.

Whilst the women stared, the men looked around as if examining the beach. When their shade moved to the side, I saw the sun much lower in the sky.

"Looks like the remains of a boat," one of them said, his accent English. Somewhere in the south; London, perhaps.

"Yes, it does," the other replied. An American. New York, or that side of the continent.

"What are you doing here? Was there anyone with you?" the blonde said, her voice soft and angelic as she leaned closer.

With no reply, I closed my eyes and tried to raise the memory.

Everything that should have been inside my head had deserted me.

Words scratched at my throat as I tried to speak.

"Don't worry," the blonde said, holding my hand. Or someone did. "Don't talk."

She looked up, saying something quietly to the group.

The men peered back down, the Englishman nodding first.

3

Throat still dry, but with the ache across my body gone, I woke without the urge to rush air into my lungs.

Lying in a bed, I stared at a white ceiling, at first not moving for fear of pain, but soon the heat under the thin sheet and curiosity got the better of me. Surprised when my nerves didn't scream with pain, I sat up, but closed my eyes as my vision swam.

A moment later I tried again, this time with more success and I looked across the pale stone walls, to the dark wooden dresser, then to a long mirror at its side and finally to a small table by the bed.

My eyes widened when I saw the bottle of water on the tabletop next to an apple and I leaned over, untwisting the cap before emptying the contents down my throat, almost in one go.

Gasping for air, I closed my eyes and savoured the liquid on my throat.

Then came the memories.

At first they were alien. Patchy images as I watched

the four beautiful people fuss around, then someone carried me over their shoulder. I felt muscles beneath me, until they lay me with such care in the back of an open-top car, where I savoured being rocked gently up and down.

After a brief journey, they offered food and drink. I took water, but I needed their help. Then fruit, the sharpness and sweet contrast of pineapple in my mouth. They removed the orange jacket, leaving me in the ragged shirt I still wore and the frayed edges of the high cut denim shorts as they put me to bed, where I fell asleep without thought.

On the dresser, a small bundle of material sat on the dark top, the pile too small to be anything but meant for the night. I swung my legs over the side of the bed, and with my feet on the cool tiles, I tried to stand.

Surprised not to fall straight back down, I remembered the apple and replaced it with the empty bottle. Taking a giant bite, I tried to remember what had happened before I woke on the beach.

There was nothing, not even names, or faces of the people I cared about. No mother. No father or siblings. No friends.

Everything gone. I waited for the panic to rise, but I kept my calm, instead peering through the window to the bright day and a luscious lawn complete with mown stripes as it led out to the beach.

Voices came from behind the dark wooden door, but they were quiet as if in another room, not standing on the other side. I felt a sudden need to meet those who'd saved my life.

Moving to the mirror, a stranger stood beyond the glass in a thin shirt only just held up, a strap on the bra snapped in two. The shorts ripped and frayed up the side.

None of it was worth saving.

After checking those on the dresser were my size, a thin nightshirt and matching shorts, I undressed whilst the person I didn't know copied my every move.

Naked, I tilted my head to the side, gathering up the strawberry blonde hair that ran just below my shoulders, twisting it around to form a bunch so I could take a closer look.

I stared at my shoulder, fingering the knotted white scar, feeling the bumps of the circle and the lack of sensation in the centre. No memories flooded back at the touch. I didn't know how it got there.

With my gaze running over my breasts, then down my athletic tummy, I followed the defined muscles to a line on the right and under my belly button. My appendix, I thought, but nothing else came with it.

My thin pubic hair was neat and trimmed. I felt the power in my toned legs. I liked what I saw, no matter that it didn't seem to belong to me.

4

Between bites of the apple, I dressed in the nightclothes, savouring the softness against my skin whilst giving only a passing thought to the hint of what I could see underneath.

Pulling open the room's dark wooden door, I stepped out, then turning away from the door across the hall, I peered left, lingering on a single empty wooden chair at the side. Looking to the right, the same gentle orange light came from both ends of the corridor, leaving me uncertain which way to head. The thought vanished when I heard a woman's soft laughter to the left.

Rounding a corner, I came out into an open plan room with a large table in the middle surrounded by eight chairs. Windows ran along the left and right walls and a group of three sofas were against the far wall, a bar in the corner to the right. Another door stood in the opposite corner.

The four beautiful creatures from the beach sat around the table, the two women one side and the men the other. None of them spotted me as I entered.

I watched as they talked, no one touching the breakfast feast of pastries, fruits and sliced meats laid out between them.

The brunette was the first to notice me, her eyebrow raising, along with her smile. The others soon followed suit, beckoning me forward.

The two guys stood. Both wore light linen trousers suits with white shirts. The women were in floral dresses which came high up on their thighs. The blonde wore red with blue accents, the brunette yellow with white detail.

"No need to stand," I said, their smiles widening, as if pleased to hear my voice.

"Take a seat." It was the American man, and he moved around to the head of the table, pulling out the seat and offering his hand to guide me over.

I smiled back, looking at each of them grinning my way and sat, my stomach urging me to eat as he poured coffee into a small mug and offered it over.

"You must be starving," the same man said as I took the cup.

"I am. Thank you," I replied as he placed a small plate in front of me. Despite the emptiness of my stomach, I just took a few grapes and pastry, nibbling at its edge here and there, not wanting to make a pig of myself whilst I was the centre of attention.

After a few moments, and as if they realised the silence, their conversation flowed again. I barely took notice of their words as they planned for what sounded like an upcoming trip. A discussion about where to stay. Which hotel had the biggest swimming pool.

"I'm Luke, by the way," the Englishman said, the American pouring more coffee as the others hushed.

I looked up from my plate, finishing a mouthful of warm pastry before nodding.

"And these two beauties are Kira," he said, pointing to the blonde. "And Sophie," he said, vaguely pointing in the brunette's direction. She raised her hand in the air and waved, beaming back.

"He's joking," said the blonde, waving her hand as if to dismiss him. "It's Aleksandra, but call me Aleks, please."

I continued nodding.

"And this here is Julius," Luke introduced.

"We're very pleased to meet you," the American replied.

"And what's your name?" Luke asked.

I looked back as I scoured my empty head, then turned to Julius, then Aleks, and finally Sophie. "I… I don't remember."

"Is that the only memory that's lost?" Luke added with a glance to Julius, who soon waved his hand in the air to dismiss the question.

"Not now. There's plenty of time later to interrogate the poor girl." They burst out laughing whilst I kept my smile. "But we have to call you something," he said, raising his eyebrows and then looked at the others.

I gazed at the table, nibbling at my lip as I tried to

think, not able to understand how I couldn't remember something so basic.

"Don't worry." It was Aleks who broke the silence. "It doesn't matter." Her cheeks bunched and I couldn't help but try to place her accent. She spoke English like a native, but there was something else in the background. Eastern European. Russian, perhaps, but only a trace as if she'd grown up around others with a much stronger inflection.

"You look like you might be a Beth?" Sophie said. I knew straight away she was from the Netherlands. She squinted, then shook her head when I didn't respond.

"Sarah?" Julius quickly added.

That didn't sound right, either.

"Laura? Gemma? Perhaps Emma?" Luke said, quickly firing the names one after the other.

I didn't move my head.

"Amy," Aleks stated; it wasn't a question. There was something to that name, a hint of recognition pinging in the back of my brain.

I nodded.

"Fabulous," she said, clapping her hands together gently as Sophie joined in.

"Well, until you remember, we'll call you Amy," Luke said.

I nodded, and he stood, Julius doing the same.

"Anyway, we have errands to run," Luke said. "We'll leave you in the ladies' very capable hands."

Aleks followed as the two men left the room the way I'd entered, but she returned, asking if I'd had enough food.

I had; well, at least as much as I wanted to eat whilst being watched. As I pushed away my plate, a man wearing a black and white suit came through the doorway at the end of the room. He carried a tray and was soon clearing away the barely touched food.

"Follow me," Aleks said, but when I turned, she'd already gone, leaving Sophie to take my hand and guide me past the chair outside the room where I'd slept.

After rounding a corner, I was in another bedroom. A giant bed stood in the middle of the far stone wall. On top of each of the two dressers along one side were a rainbow of perfume bottles. Paintings of the sea in watercolour hung on the other side.

Aleks stepped from behind a door, holding a dress high in each hand. Both were beautiful floral prints. One white and blue, the other an orangey-red.

Sophie pointed to the latter. "This one. To go with your hair."

Aleks bunched her cheeks then looked to the other dress, contemplating for a moment. "No. This one. To match your eyes." She didn't glance at Sophie, who raised her brow, then turned and left.

The dress was lovely, they both were, but I'd rather have worn a pair of jeans and t-shirt. I said nothing, instead thanking her, thinking twice about asking if she had any underwear before heading back to my room to change.

When I returned to the wide room, I found them both standing by the sofas, the table empty. At Aleks' request, I span around, but slowed as the dress's short skirt spread out.

"How are you feeling?" she asked. "You're looking a little peaky."

"I do feel groggy from the food. Can we go for a walk?" I said.

They both laughed as Sophie looked to the other woman.

"Of course," Aleks added, hooking Sophie's arm, then pulling me along with the other as we headed through the corridor and out of the front door and into the sun.

We walked barefoot, taking our time along the beach. I felt so cool in the dress, despite the beating sun.

Sometimes the two women spoke between themselves, talking about the trip, or whatever was to happen next week. Other times they asked questions, but nothing of consequence, stopping as they remembered I couldn't answer.

With each step along the beach, a steep bank ran along our side. The sand would be a tough climb, but we never deviated from the flat, staying by the lapping sea I couldn't help but stare out across. I saw no land on the horizon, no boats. It was as if we were the only people left in the world.

"What is this place?" I asked as Aleks looked at me as if to check I was okay. Her only reply was a giggle and then to turn me around by the arm so we could head back.

As we walked the other way, the subject long changed, I saw movement on top of the dune in the distance, perhaps a black figure in a green uniform, but when I looked back, they were gone and I dismissed the thought.

After what seemed like a good few hours of walking, and seeing the house's bleach white stone outside and dark pitched roof for the first time as we arrived back, there was already a jug of ice water on the table, surrounded by five glasses. Julius and Luke followed in behind us, laughing as if sharing a joke only moments before.

As they settled, Julius put his arm around Sophie's

shoulder, pulling her in close.

"How was everyone's morning?" he said, looking at Aleks and finally to me with a raised eyebrow.

The two women peered my way, their smiles urging me to answer.

"We went for a lovely little walk," I said.

"Along the beach," Sophie added.

"Where else?" Julius said, laughing as he looked to Aleks and then Luke. "I'll get chef to prepare lunch."

For a moment I couldn't help wondering what he'd meant with his first words, but when he was partway through turning toward the door at the far end of the room, he stopped and caught my attention. "Oh yes. Chef wants to make you something special tonight. What's your favourite food? You can choose whatever you like."

My eyes lit up, already so hungry.

"Fish and chips," I said, the choice coming without thought.

They all laughed, but Luke shook his head. "I think we're getting to know you just fine."

I frowned, suddenly worried I'd said something wrong.

"Don't worry," he added. "Most people wouldn't have chosen fish and chips. That's all."

"I guess you like what you like," I said with a shrug.

Nods carried around the group until Julius headed through the door at the far end.

"I'm going for a lay down," Aleks said, smiling at each of us.

"Me too," I said, feeling my own fatigue. "If that's okay?"

Aleks grinned back. "Amy, you don't have to ask. Treat this place as your own."

As she left, Luke turned to Sophie and raised his brow, then I heard his lowered voice just as I stepped into the doorway.

"How about we head off too?"

5

Refreshed from a dreamless sleep, I woke late with the sun already on its way down and I realised I must have missed lunch, my stomach growling a reminder. As I opened the door of the room, the chair still in place to the left, I smelt the unmistakeable comfort of cooked chips, then spotted Aleks walking along the corridor.

"Hey, sleepy head," she said, beaming at me. "We hoped it was you stirring. It's time for dinner."

With a skip in my step, I followed to find once again, everyone was already sitting around the table, the head set for me.

Just as Aleks sat, the man in the dark suit opened the far door, wheeling in a trolley before unloading large plates of fish and chips with mushy peas and a huge wedge of lemon on the side. He served me first whilst I looked on in awe.

"Dig in," Julius said, and I did, this time unconcerned with what they thought of my speed. I drank the wine, and then a second glass as the man who waited in the corner filled it to just below the top.

After finishing a quarter of the plate, I slowed, feeling the effects of the alcohol. Taking water, the fuzzy feeling built, and I felt myself swaying as my appetite disappeared.

Aleks spoke of the walk, Sophie of something I didn't quite catch. Luke and Julius talked of a contract almost ready to sign, and a delivery to be made in the coming days. None of them seemed to notice I'd stopped eating.

Without warning, Julius turned to me and I felt my cheeks redden at the thought of how drunk I'd become in such a short time.

"Are you enjoying the fish?" he said, smiling as the others followed to look.

"It's very nice," I said. "But I've had better." The words came out without my consent and my hand went to my mouth, but it was too late.

Laughter went around the table, everyone looking at each other and then back at me.

Mortified, I couldn't believe how rude I'd been.

"Don't worry," Luke said between fits of laughter. "We won't tell chef."

"Where on earth did you get better fish and chips?" Julius asked. "We'll have to pay a visit." The laughter rose again.

I scoured my memory, but like the rest of what must have once filled my brain, despite an eagerness to answer, there was nothing there. I shook my head, and Julius looked at Luke.

"Well, never mind. Cancel the reservation."

Only Aleks wasn't laughing; instead she stared at me, her eyes narrowed.

"So, how's the rest of your memory?" It was Julius again. "Anything come back yet?"

I wore my smile as a mask. I felt anything but happy and needed to lie down, but would do what I could not to appear rude again.

"Nothing from before I awoke on the beach." The words slurred as I spoke, but if they'd heard it, no one let on, or perhaps it was just how it sounded inside my brain. A flash of panic rose. Was it the alcohol or something else? Trauma from whatever happened before I landed on the beach?

"What's your name?" A voice said, but as I turned to the words, the colours smeared across my view, only settling when I kept my head still. Both Luke and Julius were looking at me, but I didn't know who'd spoken.

"C…" The sound came out then halted as I tried to think. "Am…" The start of my second attempt sounded right, but I tried again. "C..."

A fog seemed to fill my head, but I wasn't going to try and shake it away.

A voice interrupted my thoughts. This time, I was sure it was a woman. "That's enough. I think we need to get Amy off to bed."

"In a moment," a voice said.

"No." The word was sharp, and no more followed as I stared straight ahead, keeping my head still so I wouldn't throw up.

I closed my eyes and felt myself falling to the side.

***

Surrounded by the ocean, and in almost complete darkness, salt water stung my eyes as a wave washed over my head. With the stars so vivid, so bright, the view didn't last long as I dipped below the surface, forgetting what a bad idea it was to open my mouth.

Hands reached around me, pulling my head into the air, then dragged me along whilst I marvelled before the next wave hit, crashing over me with such force.

6

I woke, pleased to see the bedroom's stone walls bright from the moonlight. The calm faded as I realised I was desperate for the toilet.

Standing, my muscles felt strong, and with my feet firm on the cool tiled floor, I stepped across the hallway before pulling up the dress and landing on the toilet.

Savouring the relief, all need for sleep vanished. I was wide awake and couldn't bear the thought of laying in bed waiting for the dream again.

With my feet silent on the floor, although I wasn't trying to hide my steps, I came out from the bathroom and noticed the chair that had been beside the bedroom door had gone. Dismissing the thought, I followed the orange glow into the living room.

There they were. Sophie perched on a high stool at the bar, flicking through a magazine with a martini glass in her hand. Julius and Luke leaning over papers spread out on the coffee table between two of the sofas, whilst Aleks stood to the side, pointing down at something I couldn't see.

She was the first to spot me and moved away from the men as they all turned, their expressions a mixture of relief and surprise.

"How are you feeling, Amy?" Aleks said.

I nodded. "I'm so sorry about earlier," I said, looking between each of them. Their smiles told me I didn't need to worry.

"You're still recovering," Sophie said, tipping her head to the side. "You've been asleep for a day and a half."

"We were going to call the doctor if you weren't up in the morning," Aleks added, sipping from a tumbler she picked up from the bar.

"I'm fine. In fact, I feel great. So full of energy. I need to burn it off."

The two men smiled, looking at the other and laughing.

Aleks shook her head. "Boys. They're always thinking about *that*." She turned back to me. "What do you want to do?"

"What time is it? I'd like to go for a run."

Aleks raised her brow and turned to Luke and Julius. "It's about seven pm."

"Anyone want to come with me?" I added, but when Julius shrugged, Aleks placed the drink back on the bar and walked over, taking my hand and leading me to her bedroom.

Pulling out one of the dresser drawers, she moved things to the side. "For yoga," she said, handing over a sports bra, a t-shirt and a pair of cycling shorts. "They should fit you fine. But I don't have shoes."

"That's okay," I said as I took them.

Just as I was about to leave, she walked towards the door. "You can change in here. It's okay. No one will disturb you."

I nodded, then called after her. "Can I borrow some underwear?"

She stopped at the doorway, smiling back as she shook her head. "I don't own any. We're in paradise, remember." She then left the room.

I dressed and was soon back with the others. After they each looked me over, nodding as if satisfied, I turned, but twisted back around when Julius spoke.

"Just stick to the beach," he said, not lingering to see my nod as he turned back to his papers.

As I headed back out the door, I paused when part

of the dream flashed into my head, my vision filling with a dark hand on my arm as if guiding me through the water.

I wasn't alone in the sea.

7

Leaving the outside lights of the house behind, I savoured the warmth beneath my feet, despite the late hour, and stared out across the waves lapping at the shore, the gentle rhythm soon calming my thoughts.

I loved the extra effort of running in the sand, relishing the pull of my muscles working so hard. My legs felt powerful as I scoured the moonlit beach, but for what, I wasn't sure.

My mind wandered as time went on, but when a brief flash of red light out to sea caught my eye, I looked away only when a sudden pain shot up from my toe as if caught on a rogue stone.

I didn't spot the light again.

By then I must have been running for half an hour at least, but with no complaint from my body, I was eager to keep going.

Of all the questions running through my mind, I couldn't get away from the thought that I hadn't arrived alone on the beach that night. If only I knew where the four had found me, then maybe I could search, but the only place else a companion could go was over the dune, and the instructions from Julius couldn't have been clearer.

Perhaps the guiding hands were just a dream, but still I couldn't help searching for any clue that it might have been real.

Looking up the dune, a man and a woman's voice interrupted the gentle lapping of the waves. I slowed, seeing a new faint light washing up to the sky.

The two people were playfully talking and sounded as if they were just over the hill, but after a sharp rush of air, as if someone had been told to be quiet, the light went out and the voices were no more.

I pushed away the thought of looking, knowing I'd agreed to stay on the beach. The four had been so generous, it wouldn't have been fair to ignore their one rule.

Picking up the pace, I thought about turning around, but I ran on and after a few minutes I saw lights in the distance as the banking to the side flattened out with the house soon coming into focus and I realised I was on a small island.

***

I sat in a dark room with a table at my front. The walls were glass and pitch black as if it were night.

Two men were in the seats opposite. Both looked so familiar, but I didn't know why. To the left was an older guy, his face rough from old acne. The other was much younger. Both concentrated on what I was saying.

I couldn't hear the words I spoke, or their replies as I slid my hand over documents spread between us. I couldn't see their content or move my head to get a better look. The men sometimes nodding, other times their eyes wide, as if alarmed at what I said.

The vision told me nothing, other than I was on the island for a reason.

8

As I approached the side of the house, looking past an over and under garage door built into the white stone wall, I saw Aleks peering out along the way I'd started my run as she stood just outside the front door.

"Hey," I called out, and she turned to me, her eyes narrowed until she realised who'd shouted.

Luke appeared at her back, then stepped from the doorway, almost scowling, his expression softening as I arrived.

"You ran around the entire island?" she said, her head tilted to the side.

"Um. Sure. Was that okay?" I replied, only a little out of breath. "I stuck to the beach, like Julius said."

She laughed, resting her hand on her breastbone. "That's..." she said, but stopped herself and shook her head. "That's a very long way."

I shrugged. "I guess it means I'm a runner."

Luke was still looking around. "Did you see anyone on your travels?"

I shook my head. "It's like we're the only people on the island. Well, nearly."

"What do you mean, nearly?" he said, and leaned toward me.

"I didn't see them, but I heard a man and a woman talking. They weren't that far out, I don't think. I didn't go up the dune," I added but Luke didn't wait for me to finish before he went back into the house. "I promise. Did I say something wrong?"

Aleks smiled. "No. Of course not. Let's go inside."

Following her into the house and feeling a slight ache in my muscles, she guided me to the main room where the two men stood beside the table talking. I guessed

Sophie had already gone to bed.

"I'm sorry. I lost track of time," I said as they both looked at me, not hiding their uncertainty.

"We were a little worried, that's all," Luke replied, glancing at Aleks and then back.

"You just ran a half marathon," Julius said, his eyebrows raised. "In under ninety minutes."

"I guess I'm good at running."

Aleks laughed whilst Julius downed the brown contents of his glass.

With a knock at the front door, Julius headed to answer it, with Aleks following. I crossed the room, having seen a jug of iced water.

Both of them returned after a couple of minutes, and through the windows at the front of the house I saw a man in a green military uniform headed away down the path. Over his shoulder, he carried a rifle.

"You have interesting neighbours," I said to Luke, and he nodded as if not taking in what I said. "I'm off for a shower," I added and walked away, my thoughts consumed as to how I knew the weapon was a Kalashnikov AK74M.

9

Leaning back against my door as it closed, I shut my eyes, hoping to figure out how I knew about the rifle, but instead a vision greeted me and I watched myself climb the rungs of a ladder, my feet bare against the cold steel.

I opened my eyes, confused at the strange thought, then spotted a towel resting on the corner of the bed.

Picking it up, I ran my hand across the soft surface and turned, the view changing to a tight space with three shallow bunks on either side. The room rocked from side to side as if I were on a train, or a ship.

Excited, hoping these were memories, not a sign of madness, I couldn't help imagining that perhaps it was how I'd arrived here.

Soft voices in the corridor pulled me back to the moment, and after drawing a deep breath, I crossed the empty corridor. As I stepped into the bathroom, the shower was already running, the air thick with steam as I glared at the glass separator, a little surprised when I found it empty.

I undressed, then stepped under the water, savouring the heat, soothing the ache in my muscles.

Clean and refreshed, I turned off the flow just as the door opened. I was halfway out of the panel's cover when I noticed Aleks standing in the doorway. I didn't flinch or move back behind the glass panel's condensation, and with a knot in my stomach I gazed back, watching as she raised her brow and opened her mouth, her lips hinting at a smile.

I stepped out into the open so she could get the full view.

Aleks looked me up and down and I noticed the towel in her hand. Then, as if only just aware of what was happening, she broke the silence. "Sorry. I didn't realise you already had one."

"It was in the room," I replied, nodding, my voice quiet.

"*Your* room," she said, the sound of her voice electrifying my exposed skin. Aleks took a step forward, then with a distant call from Julius, she turned and left.

If I wasn't so hungry, I wouldn't have been able to resist going right to bed, but instead I dried and pulled on the dress, then headed back to the living room where

I found Julius sat at the table opposite a single cloche and a place set for dinner.

"Where is everyone?" I asked, but I only wanted to see one person.

"I am to entertain you, so it seems. The others are having an early night," he said with a raise of his eyebrows. "I hope you're hungry," he added, lifting a tumbler of golden liquid to his lips. "Luke told chef what to cook. I hope he's done a better job this time."

I eyed the cloche with mock suspicion, but slid into the chair before lifting the lid.

"Bangers and mash apparently," he said, the words sounding awkward in his accent.

"Amazing," I said, grabbing the knife and fork, soon working through the meal, unconcerned that Julius watched every mouthful.

With the plate empty, I sat back.

"Is there anything else you want?" he said, looking at my empty water glass. "Wine?"

I shook my head. "Based on how I felt last night, I don't think that's wise."

"Anything instead?"

I shrugged. "I don't know what I like."

His eyebrows rose and he stood. "Now *that* I can help with," he said, raising his finger and headed behind the bar, just as the man in the suit appeared and took my plate away.

Julius busied himself pouring from one or other of the bottles as he lined up glasses along the worktop. After a few minutes, he was back, carrying four glass tumblers on a tray, along with a single bottle of beer, then placed each of them between us.

"Let's see what you're into," he said.

"Perhaps I don't drink," I replied, raising an

eyebrow.

"I guess we're going to find out."

"But I don't want to feel like I did before," I said, haunted by the earlier experience.

"Trust me," he said, looking me in the eye. "I think you'll be fine tonight."

He pointed his open hand to the bottle of beer.

I took a swig and enjoyed the cold, refreshing taste, so took another gulp before placing it back.

The liquid in the first tumbler looked much the same rich brown as had been in his now empty glass, the strong vapours clawing at my nose as I sniffed. I grimaced at the slightest of sips, the smoky liquid seeming to burn a path down my throat.

Shaking my head, I rested the glass back in line.

"That's a five-hundred-dollar bottle of scotch," he said, laughing, then took the glass, replacing it with his own.

The next looked like water. The smell was raw, but familiar and I let a drop touch my tongue, then downed the rest.

"You drink vodka then," he said, raising his glass.

I nodded, savouring the lightness of my head, which felt so much different to how I'd been last night.

The third glass was a similar colour to the first. I eyed it with suspicion. "It's not whiskey again, is it?"

He shook his head. "No. Try it."

I smelt the sweet vapour as I drew it to my mouth, then tipped back my head for a proper taste. It was like nectar, bringing with it memories of standing in a bar amongst a large group. They were all men. A row of spirit bottles lined the bar top, and we toasted, knocking back the glass to raucous cheers as someone refilled us from a full bottle.

"Are you okay?" Julius said, pulling me back into the room. "Are you remembering?"

I paused for a moment. "Rum?"

He nodded, turning up the corner of his mouth.

"We stole a bottle from my parent's drinks cabinet as a teenager," I said, unsure why I'd told the lie.

"Didn't we all?" he said, then nodded to the last glass, also filled with a clear liquid.

With a sniff, I shook my head and placed it back down. "I'm not even going to taste that one."

"Tequila," he said with a raise of his brow. "And it's probably for the best."

He stood, motioning to the sofas. "I'll get you some more rum whilst you make yourself more comfortable."

I did as he asked, sitting on the over-stuffed seat and he soon joined me, passing a refilled glass of the brown liquid.

"When does your holiday end?" I said as he sat beside me on the edge of the cushion so he could look at me, his knee touching mine.

"This isn't a holiday," he said, and for a moment I thought perhaps I'd offended him, but his bright expression didn't waver.

"You must be important people. Or rich," I said.

He laughed, leaning back and then forward again.

"We're each important in our own way."

"Sure, but some people are more important than others. Not everyone gets to live on an island and have such a beautiful partner," I said, ending the word high, as if with a question.

"Aleks is not my partner," he said without a breath. "She's my..." he said, but stopped as he thought about what he should say. "A friend."

I raised my eyebrows, speaking slowly, unsure if I

should say the words. "Maybe a little more than a friend?"

His cheeks bunched. "Now and then," he replied. "We have an understanding, and it goes both ways."

"And she knows that?" I replied, realising how it might sound, but before I could worry, he answered.

"Of course."

I waited a little before I said anything more, despite having so many questions.

"So, do you see many other people?" I finally said.

"I never kiss and tell."

I gulped down the rum, my eyes widening as I welcomed the feeling.

"Can I kiss you?" he said, his words taking me by surprise, as did my reply.

"Yes."

I watched as he leaned in.

The kiss felt okay, not unpleasant, but I didn't move in for more, nor did I back away.

He stood and took my hand. I followed as he led me through the corridor to the door of the bedroom where Aleks had given me her clothes, and there she was, sat up in the middle of the bed, her bottom half under a sheet, her top half naked as she read a book.

"Look who I've brought with me," Julius said.

Aleks let the book down, biting her bottom lip.

That's when the fire ignited inside me.

10

It was morning when I woke laying between Julius and Aleks, muscles aching in places it felt as if I rarely exercised. I smiled at the memories of Aleks keeping me to herself, telling Julius he was in for a treat as she tied his hands to the chair.

The treat, it turned out, was for me.

Aleks and I played for what seemed like hours as Julius could only watch. Despite his obvious desire to join in, he didn't once complain whilst she taught me things I was pretty sure hadn't just vanished with my other memories.

When his time came, it was my turn to watch on the edge of the bed, but I didn't need restraining to keep away whilst Aleks made sure he had no energy to come after me.

I sat up, careful not to disturb either of them, although I longed to put my hand under the covers and wake her without a word, until I remembered the flashbacks and last night's incoherent dreams.

I had to clear my head.

Still naked, and taking great care as I shuffled up to sit on my pillows, I stood, vaulting over Aleks and landing on the floor at the side of the bed before hurrying off to my room, not bothering to find where they'd discarded my dress. After pulling on the running things from last night, I was out the door with the fresh morning air in my face.

Despite the miles of sand under my feet as I stared along the unending horizon, the sun glistening on the calm sea, I couldn't shake the thought that I'd come to this place for a reason. How, I didn't know, or why.

Those questions were still to be answered and I couldn't help but think the solutions might wait on the other side of the dune.

I'd decided in an instant and turned inland, my pace slowing as I climbed up the steep bank, struggling to get purchase with the sand falling away under my feet.

Eventually I stood at the top and watched the mound fall to the other side before it levelled out, perhaps with tyre tracks, and then it climbed again with a dune much larger than the first.

Having made the decision, I wouldn't let a small hill turn me around and I was down the other side, pumping my legs harder every moment, rising until my head crested the highest point where I found what I thought I must have been looking for.

11

Staring down a dusty airstrip disappearing into the distance, I stood at the far end, close to a handful of shacks and sheds. Just beyond stood the imposing bulk of a large transport aircraft, a venerable C130 Hercules with the USAF lettering still hinting on the faded paintwork.

A fuel truck parked at its side with a hose snaking into the fuselage via a propped hatch. A shiver run down my spine, but I didn't know why my body reacted like that.

The large loading door at the back of the aircraft stood open as figures in desert camouflage pushed hand carts laden with dark green crates on top.

Munitions; I knew without any thought.

Ducking low, I realised I couldn't stay where I was for fear those walking around would see me. I climbed over the crest, then slid down the bank, jogging to the side of the nearest shack, and pressed my back against the heat of the wooden building.

With a sudden uncertainty of what I should do next as I stared back at the dune, I thought of running away before someone spotted me. About to climb back up, the rhythmic stomp of boots on the tarmac and distant engines caused me to stop.

I peered around the wood to a convoy of cars followed by a truck as they drove down the runway towards the aircraft.

Transfixed, I watched the black cars at the head, then looked at the large group of men dressed in military fatigues marching their way. They soon met and stopped, the cars halting between two parallel lines formed by the men.

I could just about make them out as they stood to attention, still watching as four figures came from the cars, then others from around the back of the truck.

For a moment, I thought they dragged something along the ground behind them.

Unsure what I was looking at, the four men gathered between the two lines of troops, and waited as the soldiers from the truck pulled whatever it was with them.

I squinted, but couldn't make out any more detail.

An incoherent shout called out, echoing across the flat ground but lost of all its meaning.

I was about to lean forward to see if I could get closer when I heard a call from right behind me and felt a hand on my shoulder.

12

Without the need to see who it was, my body took over and I reached across my chest, grabbing hold of warm fingers whilst I span on the spot. Yanking the hand closer, and before I'd seen anything other than a black guy in army fatigues, I'd pulled his hand down, grabbing the back of his head with my other arm and forcing it to smash against my knee.

The man stumbled back, and I stepped to follow, curling my hands behind his head again, then crashing his skull into my knee for a second time. He went limp, and I looked around, my breath settling when I saw there was no one else around.

I felt no regret as I looked at the figure crumpled on the tarmac, and I bent, taking the AK74 from his shoulder and unclipping the magazine before checking the empty chamber. Pulling off the metal dust cover, I had the recoil spring out, followed by the piston and bolt a moment after, then scattered the components around him.

Grabbing the man by the shoulders, I had him up, being careful not to spill the blood from his nose on my clothes, and pushed him away to lay flat on his back. A pair of binoculars hung around his neck and a holster rested on his right hip. I thought about taking the pistol, but knew one shot would be enough to alert the entire island.

At the sound of a gunshot, I grabbed the binoculars, pushing them to my eyes as I peered around the shack. Focusing on a body dressed in white slumped at Luke's feet, Julius stood beside him and watched as Luke turned, holding a pistol at a soldier's forehead, then pulled the trigger.

Memories cascaded into my head.

In the dark room, I'd been with Franklin and Clark. The scattered files were photos of Julius, some of Luke. The maps were of the African nation of Togo, and a tiny island just off the coast, the entire surface of which was the base of a militia army.

Julius, real name Julian Rivera, was an arms dealer

turned right-hand man of the tyrannical leader of Togo. For years he'd lined his pockets feeding the civil war, but now someone powerful had grown tired of the toothless international process which should have made the terrible acts impossible.

Julius, and his life-long friend Luke, were linked with the death of hundreds of thousands, but there were likely millions more that hadn't been counted.

Despite this, he kept to himself, barely in the limelight and shrouded in mystery, his history potted with false names and legends. He was so afraid of exactly what I was here to achieve.

Attempts had been made before, but each had been betrayed.

Snatch squads. Lone operatives. Snipers. All tried. Each time they'd been given up, some with reports that the operators had surrendered, revealing their task to the man himself.

In the room, we'd guessed a lie detector, or truth drug, perhaps, and we'd been right, now knowing it wasn't the wine that had made me feel bad after all.

The operation had to be deniable, and with the small army protecting him, an overt offensive was off the cards. It called for a special someone, inserted to befriend him. I'd go in by submarine, but it was me that suggested they take away my memory, at least for a few days.

Franklin called the plan madness, but I told him there was no other way. He suggested no better option. Even as I stood on top of the submarine's conning tower in the bright orange life jacket, the Royal Navy doctor gave me a chance to back out, reminding me she had no idea how long it would take for my memory to come back, and that it might all flood in, taking me by surprise, or it perhaps be months before I remembered everything about who I was.

I could fall unconscious, unable to breathe in the water, so I suggested the two Special Boat Service swimmers guide me along the half mile to the beach. The scattered debris was Clark's idea.

Staring through the binoculars, I watched the pair move back to the car, then drive away, leaving the two bodies slumped on the tarmac.

I wondered if they'd announced the reasons for the deaths. Perhaps they'd broken some rule, or maybe they were just setting an example. Or were they the man and woman I'd overheard yesterday?

It no longer mattered. The reign of terror was ending today.

13

I ran, this time as fast as I could manage, and all the while I kept my mind clear, doing my best not to pre-empt what I'd find back at the house. Instead, I wallowed in my memories, the good and the not so. There were plenty of each.

When the house came into view, I slowed, and I was through the door and into the main room, finding it empty, Julius and Luke not back from the airfield.

The table was set for four places, but the breakfast was yet to be laid out.

"Hello," I called, my shout echoing against the stone as I couldn't help but wonder whose place wasn't set.

"You're back." Aleks' voice floated in from the corridor behind me, beaming a smile. "How was the run? You were much quicker this time."

"I've remembered everything. I know who I am," I replied, not holding back the joy the memories that made me who I was were not gone forever.

"That's wonderful," she said, her eyes wide with delight. "So come on," she quickly added as she swept up to me, grabbing my hands, then drawing me towards the end of the room to take a seat on the sofa.

I perched on the edge facing her, just as she did with me.

"Tell me everything. Tell me who you are."

"She's trouble."

Julius's voice came from behind us and I turned to see him coming through the doorway, Luke following.

I stood, Aleks doing the same when we saw the black Walther P99QA in his hand, pointing at my chest.

"Do tell," Aleks said, her voice calm, but I resisted turning to her.

"We were taking care of business," he said, Aleks nodding in the corner of my vision as she listened. "And just as we were driving away, we were called back with reports a guard had been attacked."

"Attacked?" Aleks said. "Is he okay?"

"He's busted up pretty good," Julius said, not looking away from me.

"And you think our guest is responsible?" Her voice rose as if unsure how it could be true. "She hadn't lied."

"How many people on the island have hair like that?" he replied, jabbing the pistol toward my head. "A guard spotted her climbing back over the dune."

In the periphery of my vision, Aleks moved, disappearing around my back, but I held my ground, knowing to do anything else would show my hand. Then, just as she came around the other side, Julius's gaze moved from me to her.

I took my chance.

With a step back, I twisted, sweeping up a plate from the dining table at my side before sending it through the air like a frisbee.

The plate hit Julius square in the throat, then crashed to the tiles. He reached for his neck, dropping the gun and I lurched forward, sweeping the pistol from the floor before bringing his elbow down to my knee, pleased with the sickening crack.

I span away in case he could muster a counterattack, but he fell to his knees, consumed by the shock. Luke froze on the spot, staring down the barrel.

Aleks had stopped moving, her face pale as I glanced over. She was a couple of arm's lengths away to my right, and for a moment I thought she might faint.

"They're bad people Aleks. They took two lives on the airstrip and they've killed so many more," I said, rushing out the words.

Aleks shook her head, her hands on her cheeks. "What?" she said. "I don't understand... Who the hell are you?"

"I'm someone with a job to do," I replied.

"What job?" she quickly added as she looked between me and Julius, still writhing on his knees.

I took two shots, one to each of the men's heads to give her the answer.

14

"Come with me," I said, giving the bodies no time to settle on the tiles.

Aleks stood with her hand across her mouth, her eyes wide as she stared at the two dead men and their spreading blood.

"Where's Sophie?" I asked when she didn't respond. "She should come too. I can get you both away from this place, but we have to go now."

"Where?" was all she could say as she shook her head.

"Anywhere but here. They'd have heard the gunshot. Is there a car in the garage?"

She shook her head. "A boat."

"Even better," I replied, raising my brow. "Are you coming?"

When she still hadn't spoken, I stepped toward her, placing the pistol on the table and gripped both her upper arms, giving her a gentle shake.

After a moment, she looked me in the eye but soon turned to the gun.

I shook her again.

"Aleks. We have to go. Where is Sophie?" I asked.

Aleks shook her head. "She was with Julius," she said, her voice quiet.

"Shit," I replied then released her, picking up the weapon and raising my voice. "Sophie," I called out.

Suddenly my mind was back on the runway, looking down through the binoculars, desperate to see if it was Sophie lying dead before they'd killed the other.

Still shaking my head I knew there was no time to find out, and I gripped Aleks' hand, dragging her through the house and out into the sun. We were soon along the front of the building, letting her go only as I came up to the garage door, where I gripped the handle tight, twisting in hope it was unlocked.

With relief, it turned. With your own private army for security, why would you worry about thieves, I guessed. Inside, sitting on a metal framed trailer with a single wheel on either side, was a grey rigid inflatable with an outboard engine at the rear.

I threw the gun inside the hull and, releasing the handbrake, I pulled it out of the garage, dragging it along the front of the house, before calling for Aleks' help as I slid it from the trailer.

With a glance back to the house, there was still no sign of any arrivals, but a cloud of dust in the background told me they wouldn't be long.

"My things," Aleks said at my side.

"Leave them," I replied, my voice firm as I shook my head. "They're no good for you now. It's time to leave this all behind."

She stared toward the house as I shuffled the boat into the water.

"A clean slate?" she said in almost a whisper.

With a nod as she turned to me, she took my offered palm, and I helped her into the boat. With the water lapping at my navel, I pushed away until it floated.

The engine started with the first pull of the cord, and with Aleks sitting on the side of the inflatable, I turned the handle. We soon gathered speed, the boat bouncing across the waves as I glanced behind for the last time. The house would soon be too small to make out any new arrivals.

Staring at the back of her head, I watched as Aleks gazed at the horizon, but with the wind in my face, I couldn't get her earlier words out of my head.

A clean slate.

Snapshots from the last few days played out in my mind.

Aleks perched on the edge of the sofa as Luke and Julius talked late at night.

Aleks and Julius greeting the soldier together at the

door.

It was Aleks who gave the permission, to run, to call the space my room. For everything. And it was her bedroom, not shared.

Julius hadn't put up a fight last night, despite being keen enough to take his turn.

The breakfast table only set for four.

They hadn't known about me yet, so it must have been Sophie they knew wouldn't be coming back. "You knew," I said and Aleks turned and looked at me, shaking her head. "She went out with the boys. I didn't see her come back."

"Was she sleeping with a soldier?" I blurted out.

"I don't know what you mean?" Aleks replied, looking away, but the thought wouldn't leave my head. It was all so obvious now.

Aleks was in charge.

"A clean slate from what?" I asked.

She looked at me, her expression so relaxed.

"Julius was a mask. Wasn't he?" I said, but couldn't help bursting into laughter. "Well, I'm all for girl power. Damn."

Her eyes narrowed just a little, then she smiled, her cheeks bunching. "No one ever suspects the pretty woman."

"And Sophie?"

She scoffed and looked away again. "Just a bimbo that couldn't keep her hands off the hired help," she replied, shaking her head. "There's only one way off this island."

Looking as if she was about to say something, Aleks held back as movement in the water caught our attention, a post rising a few car lengths away.

"For most," I said, leaning forward to pick up the

gun. Feeling its weight in my grip, I raised it and pulled the trigger, watching as she soon disappeared into the water.

With a shake of my head, I realised I'd done it again. I'd broken the rule I'd set myself early in my career. But I'd had an excuse this time, having no memory of my promise never to sleep with the enemy.

Nodding to myself, I dropped the gun over the edge, then dived into the water on the other side of the boat just as I saw the rising bridge fin of the Trafalgar Class submarine.

With my palms on the dark hull, I climbed the rope ladder strung to the side, nodding to the man dressed in combat fatigues with no rank designation on his epaulets. At his back, the doctor rose up the ladder.

"Who are you?" she said as I climbed in.

I grinned.

"I'm Agent fucking Carrie Harris."

Discover more of Agent Carrie Harris in Operation Dawn Wolf available on Amazon or check out **www.gjstevens.com** for signed copies.

Beginning of the End

1

Wedged in the tight space, I stood shivering; not just because of the cold on my bare arms or piercing through my thin pyjamas. Not because of the darkness; the only light coming from the bottom of the door. Not for the memory of that smell that made me want to gag with every breath.

My stomach gripped tight, like a hand clenched around my organs, but not only because I hadn't finished my breakfast. There was plenty of food stacked on the long rows of shelves on the other side of the door, but only if I cared to chance my life with what might be waiting beyond.

I shook because the once blaring sirens had gone silent, along with the other loud noises that faded to nothing. I shook for what would come next.

I'd been there so long. Hours at least. Half a day, perhaps. My bladder aching.

I was in a cupboard; a utility room barely seen in the flash of daylight as I ran in. Pulling the door closed behind me, I panted so hard I thought I would burst. I'd seen the shelves, but not paid attention to their colourful contents. I'd seen the great white porcelain sink I leaned against and the mop and bucket in the corner. I smelt the stale odour.

Despite knowing I could turn and relieve myself in the sink, I couldn't bring myself to expose my back to the door and let my guard down to relieve the pain.

A not-too-distant sound of feet scraping along the pavement beyond the outer door stopped me just as the courage rose enough for the turn.

The sound died back and I relaxed, but not enough to move from the spot. Not enough to twist around and take those few moments to risk my life for a little discomfort.

The shivering grew worse, each tremor as if it would force my aching bladder to burst.

I slowly raised my hands, pausing at what could have been a sound beyond the door, or it could have been my imagination; an imagination I hoped had made this all up. An imagination which had conjured the fear, the pain and the loss.

I strained to hear, but the sound had gone and I tried not to think of something heavy, a body, being dragged across the floor. I tried not to think of my brother out there. And my mum.

It had been long enough; the moments sinking into memories. The feelings overtaking the sights. Everything twisted in my mind. They could have been out there searching for me. They could have been waiting to explain the misunderstanding. To tell me I'd been sleepwalking. To tell me I shouldn't have run off. To say I shouldn't have followed Mum's plea to get away.

Not able to hold back any longer, I eased my hands backwards. Feeling the cold of the sink, I rushed around, pulling my thin trousers down. Breathing away the relief, I clenched at the sound it made gurgling down the plughole. It smelt so strong, so rich. Mum's voice reminded me I had to drink more.

Pulling up my trousers, I basked in the comfort and my mind wandered back to her voice ringing in my ears.

"Run."

2

Steve, my brother, worked long hours; usually leaving before I woke and would be back home just as Mum served dinner.

Yesterday, staggering through the door and arriving much earlier than he normally would, he surprised me, almost sending me falling into the Christmas tree and spilling my lunch across the floor.

On seeing his grim expression and grey complexion, I spoke whilst trying not to show my concern over his hunched appearance.

"Are you okay?"

"Sure," he replied, squinting as he shuffled over to the fridge before opening the door to glance at the shelves.

"You don't look it," I said.

"I'm fine."

"What's wrong with your arm?" I added, as I noticed he'd kept it bent at the elbow and tucked in front of his stomach.

"Nothing," he replied, turning his back as he pulled out a carton of orange juice and drank.

"You could get a pay-out," I said and he turned, scowling my way. "What did your work say about it?"

"Nothing," he said, glaring at me before dropping the juice carton back on the shelf. "There's bigger things going on in the world than money."

"You should have told them at least."

"What does a sixteen-year-old know?" he said, still with his back to me.

I turned away, listening as he staggered to the stairs, taking his time with each step until the sound faded to nothing.

When Mum came home from work, she found him sound asleep when she took in his dinner, calling me in to see if I agreed with her concern. I thought he looked much better as he slept in the double bed, thinking he probably had the cold currently going around.

It was no surprise he was ill, Mum would always say whenever he got even a sniffle. The lab worked him like a dog, especially in the run up to Christmas. I paid little attention, remembering how he'd spoken to me, and stayed focused on the TV. Mum soon switched to reminding me of the exams waiting for me when I went back to school.

They were only mocks and I had the whole of the next week to find enough enthusiasm to hit the books hard. At least that's what I thought.

I woke early the next morning and sat on the sofa, staring at the decorations we'd put up only the other day; the tired-looking tree standing in the corner of the room barely decorated. Mum never did as much since Dad died, even though he always had the least enthusiasm to cover the rooms in shiny coloured plastic.

The loading screen of the console caught my eye as I stuffed in another mouthful of cereal. My attention drew away to the sound of someone stepping down the stairs in a disjointed rhythm.

It was Steve, the last person I expected to see, and he ignored my stare as he stumbled around the house as if getting ready to go to work, despite the stoop and with his right hand tucked in his shirt like a makeshift sling. He stank as if he'd been to the toilet in his trousers. If it wasn't for him walking around, his white, drained skin would have told me he'd died in his sleep.

Despite shrugging at the thought, I couldn't completely ignore him to concentrate on the screen and the pixelated zombies I needed to shoot before they hit me.

If Steve killed himself for the government, then who was I to say anything different?

Okay, I was secretly a little worried, but I'd never tell him that. Anyway, he didn't look in the mood for anything I might have to say.

Leaving him to crash around the house, I only looked away from a great headshot as he stumbled out the front door. Guilt rose through me when I thought about him driving in such a state, hoping he'd get himself together before he drove away.

Mum must have heard the door and her footsteps rushed down the stairs.

Quickly hiding the white controller and switching the TV to the news, I settled back on to the sofa.

Whilst fastening the top buttons of her blue work tunic, she stumbled into the room, looking my way.

"Are you going to get dressed today?" she said, but instead of waiting for my shoulders to shrug, she peered around the room with her brow furrowed and rushed to ask if the sound had been Steve leaving.

"He's going to work," I said, watching her face flash with concern. I shrugged when she asked how he looked.

Sighing when I didn't speak, she shook her head.

We weren't close, my brother and I. He didn't get me and I didn't understand him.

He was some super-smart scientist living with me and Mum, back from university and sleeping in my bed, forcing me into the old box room.

His room was the biggest after Mum's and when Steve left four years ago, I took my rightful space. Why should he get the bigger room when he only came back every few months and should have moved out when he finished his course?

But no, he went off for training at a place only a few miles down the road and couldn't afford to rent a house of his own so early in his new scientific career. Mum buckled; she loved us being so close and he got the room back with a quick bat of his eyelids. That old trick.

But then again, none of that mattered anymore.

"He's just left," I said. "You might catch him if you're that worried."

Mum headed to the door to the sound of an engine revving on the drive.

I stood, knocking over the cereal bowl full of milk I'd rested on the floor. As I turned down to the mess, I held back from swearing when we heard the crunch of metal from outside.

Ignoring the spreading white puddle on the carpet, I walked behind Mum with her hand on the door. Trying to stifle my smile, I knew how much trouble the golden boy would be in when I saw his car embedded in the side of a Ford Focus.

The driver of the Focus was already out and rushing around to inspect the damage. Steve remained motionless, despite the growing tirade the guy whose car he'd hit shouted as he pointed in my brother's direction with a reddening face.

As I rushed forward with Mum squealing at the sight, I watched the guy's eyes bulge, gasping as he arrived at the window.

"No," Mum shouted, but I grabbed her hand, holding her back as the driver rushed to pull at Steve's door.

The door opened, and with relief I watched Steve sit up. A cry of pain called out, but I couldn't tell who'd made the noise as the Focus driver staggered back, holding his own arm with Steve pulling himself from the car.

Letting go of Mum, we stepped forward and watched Steve fall on top of the driver as if he'd tripped. Then came the sound of an animal's pained call.

Neighbours rushed out to the source of the noise and I watched as each reared back. A few turned and headed inside their houses. I imagined them running for their phones, others stopping, calling out for whatever was happening the other side of the car to end.

A guy in a T-shirt, Dave from number forty-eight, was the only one to come forward. He arrived before we came around the car, bending down and straining as if to pull something up.

Somehow I knew it would be my brother he was trying to pull away from whatever he was doing to the poor man.

As we circled to come around the car, Dave let out a yelp, stepping back. Blood dripped to the ground as he held his arm up. We saw Steve crouched over the driver of the Focus who lay motionless.

Mum bounded forward before I could grab her. I stayed put with indecision, my brain not able to compute the sight. I called out as she grabbed Steve by the shoulders, hysterical, screaming, calling as if she was in dire pain.

Her sound changed in an instant. She stopped her wailing, looking at the blood trickling from a wound on her hand. She staggered backwards, stumbling as she tried to slow, but landed on her bum on the road.

Everything seemed to stop.

She went silent, as if the fall had knocked out all her breath. I couldn't bring myself to look at where Steve still leaned on all fours over the Focus driver.

Mum stared my way, her eyes wide and bloodshot. She called out with a shrill wail.

"Run! Just run!"

I turned to look at Steve and he glared back with blood smeared around his mouth and down his white shirt.

As more people streamed from their houses, rushing to encircle the scene, I ran away to the sound of Mum's weakening voice.

"Run!"

3

I kept on running, knowing help would take a long time to get to our sleepy backwater, which had a visit from the police maybe once a year. Crime had always passed us by; like life, I used to think. Somewhere in the back of my mind I seemed to remember the charity box going missing from the bar at the Old Crow Inn. It was the talk of the village for weeks.

In my early teens I'd wanted to move to somewhere with more excitement, somewhere where the most interesting event wasn't the roof blowing off the church two years ago, almost killing half the parish council.

Now I'd give anything to go back to that quiet place and hold the Xbox controller in my hand.

With my breath pumping hard, it was as if I could still hear Mum calling in the distance. Her words weren't to draw me close, but to make sure I still ran away as fast as I could.

I followed the long line of houses sweeping around

the village before turning down a side street by the Mabel family's house to stop and wait, listening to the screams joining Mum's call.

The sound grew too much for me to listen to and I picked up the pace again, crossing between the houses to the road bisecting the village. I slowed, staring at the flow of more people rushing to the sounds, their eyes wide with concern and mobile phones to their ears.

I watched Dan Spence leave Cowithick's only shop, a newsagent with a tiny post office, and I stopped, my mum's distant call holding me from rushing with what looked like the rest of the village as they headed toward the terrifying sounds.

It wasn't long before I was on my own, the noise still so loud I couldn't pick out her voice amongst the others anymore. Holding my hands to my ears as if the drums were about to burst, the calls just went, silencing as if someone had flicked a switch.

I waited for the stream of people to return. I waited for what seemed like an age for everyone to head back to their houses and for someone to give me an explanation; to tell me it was all going to be okay.

But no one returned. People didn't file back. The owner of the shop, Dan Spence, didn't head through the newsagent's door he'd left wide-open in his hurry.

I couldn't help thinking perhaps everything was okay. Perhaps they were each standing around drinking coffee whilst they sorted out the mess. Perhaps comforting Steve, the driver of the Focus too, and hugging Mum.

With the terrible shouts falling silent, I convinced myself normality had returned. The panic, the nightmare, was over.

Taking slow steps, I retraced the route to peer

around the corner of the Mabel family's place to the empty street, the only unusual features of which were the open front doors of a few houses. If it wasn't for the early hour, the last time I'd checked it was just gone eight, even that wouldn't have been so unusual.

I looked down at my sweat-soaked pyjamas and couldn't help wondering if I'd just woken from a terrible dream.

After walking along the street shivering for a few moments, I picked up the pace. Our house was around the sweeping bend and I half expected to see it had all been a trick of my mind. I'd walk back and knock on the door, but there'd be no one to answer because they'd both be at work.

With growing annoyance at my mind playing such tricks, I imagined a day of hanging around the village in my pyjamas, freezing cold.

I turned the corner, jumping close to the front wall of a house as I saw Steve stumbling along in the middle of the road. Then I spotted his untucked white shirt covered in splashes of blood.

I turned away, running back down the side of the Mabels' house and across the road, through the newsagent's open door, dashing between the aisles to the tiny room at the end and shutting myself away as I checked with a last glimpse that no one followed.

As my breathing slowed, the sound of police sirens rose in the background, building my excitement with every moment. About to leave the dark confines and rush to the arriving cars, calling out all that had happened before submitting myself to their protection, I stopped, pulling back from the handle as the screams rose in the air once more.

The sirens silenced moments later.

They stayed quiet for such a long while, the stillness of the air only broken by the occasional disorderly footstep, which lacked the normal rhythm of one foot in front of the other.

New sirens came, but they were different this time. Their high tones were soon dashed with gunfire, the sound of each shot rattling through my chest and sending my body into a shiver I thought would never stop.

Pushing myself deeper into the tight space, I tried not to think of the police with their guns, powerless to stop themselves being overwhelmed. But overwhelmed by what?

I tried not to replay the earlier scenes, but couldn't stop the vision of my mother calling me to run as her blood dripped to the road. There had to be a rational cause.

Contaminated water. A chemical leak upstream of the river had somehow entered the taps. Mum would always say I didn't drink enough. Perhaps it's what saved my life. But what chemical could send someone, everyone, into a violent craze? It hadn't been covered in the study for my exams.

A cloud of toxic dust, perhaps? I hadn't been out in the open for a week, happy to play on the Xbox with the house empty of those at work.

Could either of those have sent my brother mad, filling him with such rage to become a psycho? But that wasn't the Steve I knew coming around the corner with the same intent, the same hunger for violence clear in his narrowed eyes.

Perhaps they'd all drunk the water or breathed in the gas. What about Mum? Or me? How could I be the only one not affected?

Maybe I'd just seen what I'd wanted to. Maybe I'd been playing too many video games and this was what Mum meant when she said they were no good for me. Had I crossed out of the actual world and into some other? Perhaps locked away in a reality just in my head?

Opening my palm, I slapped myself on the cheek, but it barely stung. With a second shot, harder this time, I could only just hold back the yelp as the pain radiated across my cheek. I was awake. I couldn't be surer.

The heat inside the cupboard had built and the walls seemed to close in. My elbow banged against something to the right, as if to emphasise my point. I couldn't stay in there forever, but I had no idea what I would see the other side of the door, or what crazed lunatic would see me first.

And what would I do when I left the place?

I'd run. I'd head out of the village. I'd leave the newsagent, checking through the windows first. If the coast was clear I'd run left, out of the door, past the pub and leg it to the main road around two miles away. It would take half an hour if I could keep a good pace. After running across the fields, I'd flag someone down from the road and I could find the police and tell them everything. I'd tell them to prepare.

I tried not to think they'd already know. I tried not to think since arriving in Cowithick the dispatchers wouldn't have heard from their officers. They'd send more help. They'd keep sending more people until they'd dealt with the mess. They'd send in the army if they had to.

Perhaps it was already okay. Perhaps I'd walk out to police officers searching for survivors. But why couldn't I hear them calling out?

Pushing out my hand and wrapping my fingers

around the cold handle, a vision of Steve's arm jumped into my head. I remembered the way he'd held it when he came home, and in the morning too. But when we saw him outside, it was as if nothing had happened to it. He'd used both to hit and claw out at the guy on the ground.

Had he fallen at work or burnt himself on something caustic?

A dog barked in the distance. Perhaps something had bitten him? But what?

Whatever it was, I had to get away from this place. Light flooded in as I twisted the handle and pushed, peering past the shelves and out to the street, focusing on the police car with the driver's door open and the blue lights strobing across the view.

4

Grabbing Snickers and other chocolates from the shelf as I passed, I stepped slowly through the aisles with the chill air from outside raising goosebumps on my arms. Not able to look away from the police car since I'd emerged, I realised the danger of staring and pulled myself from the trance to look left and right through the large window in search for who had driven the car.

There was no sign.

I looked further to the right and caught sight of a coat around the back of the chair at the till. I leaned over the counter, grabbing the black jacket. It smelt of old smoke. It smelt of Dan Spence and his thin, hand-rolled cigarettes. His short beard hairs scattered across the front, but it was warmer than my thin top and gave me a place to stash more chocolate and crisps.

Peering past the door, I looked to the left. Searching along the curve of the street, it was empty of people, either normal looking or deranged. Some driveways still had cars. Was that normal? It had been a few years since I'd been out this early in the holidays.

Front doors stood open. Every other one, at least. But there were no people around. No one rushing to my aid or calling out that everything had turned out okay.

To the right was much the same, although the curve was shallower. That way was the route to our house and somewhere I knew I'd regret going.

I didn't know where I should head, but I knew I had to get away and find help.

Stepping back from leaning out, I peered to the police car. Its lights distracted me with their strobing blue, but a thought came to mind; could the keys be inside? Could I figure out how to drive from what I'd seen Mum do so many times? It was only a year before I'd be doing it for real.

No. It was just an easier way to get killed or injured. I rushed from the doorway, heading over the road and back down the alley, out along the street made up of two rows of houses facing each other in a ring around the village.

I didn't look to either side, my quick pace turning to a flat-out run. Soon I arrived to where our street met the road running right through the village and cutting the ring of houses in two.

Something made me slow before I came to the new tarmac; before I passed the houses to expose myself to whatever could be on either side.

I'd been right to slow.

Standing in the middle of the road, just back from the junction whilst leaving the houses on either side as a shield, I looked along the road heading out of the village to my left. A small group of soldiers in gas masks stood with long rifles looking across the view. Behind them were two Land Rovers parked at angles to block the road.

Despite the elation of seeing the saviours in green and brown camouflage, I didn't run towards them waving my arms. Behind the soldiers and their four by fours, green army trucks with small robot-like arms mounted behind the cab headed our way, the line snaking down from the hill in a long convoy I couldn't see the end of.

I watched as the first arrived at the roadblock, diverting off to the grass, bouncing up and down as they ignored the hedges, smashing through undergrowth to move around the side of the village.

The truck behind split off, heading the opposite way. The one behind did the same, each taking it in turns to go the opposite way to the one in front. On the bed of the trucks were large flat loads stacked up high on most, but every so often the cargo would be different, instead carrying large grey boxes.

As I watched, entranced at the flowing line, I saw a pair of trucks rock to a stop on either side of the roadblock. Two soldiers jumped out of each cab, then used the stowed arm to lift what looked like sheets of metal from the flatbed at the back. The one behind did the same, unloading the concrete cubes as more soldiers with rifles slung over their shoulders guided the loads to the grass.

They weren't acting strange or erratic. Perhaps the gas masks protected them from a toxic cloud or they hadn't drunk the contaminated water.

About to rush over, waving my arms, out of the corner of my eye I saw movement, then heard a call. A woman; for a moment she was Mum. Same height, with a plump belly, but when I looked to the blonde hair down to her shoulders, the illusion vanished. She was someone else's mum running towards the soldiers, waving her hands and calling out with such joy in her voice.

I let out a breath, relaxing from the initial disappointment, and raised my hands, about to call out so they could save me as well. But as I did, I turned, watching one of soldiers walking forward with his gun aimed in her direction. After a few steps, I heard a deep but muffled command.

I lowered my hands and something in my head made me take a step back to the cover of the brickwork. The rest of the soldiers stopped what they were doing, instead swinging their rifles from their shoulders to aim at the woman.

If they'd seen what I had, they were right to take care. They were right to slow her down and check her out before getting her to safety.

A loud crack shocked my ears, then a second, third and countless more rang out as I lurched backward to the shadow of the houses to my left for cover.

Leaning into the brick whilst I edged forward, I watched puffs of blood pop into the air as the woman reeled back with each shot until she collapsed to the road.

But how could this have happened? Was I still in England?

It had always been a place of democracy. Of policing by consent, according to my social studies class.

We weren't in some third-world nation run by despots who hired mercenaries to do their evil deeds.

I felt my blood chill as I stared at the body.

Could the infection be bad enough that the only option was to kill us all rather than risk the rest of the country? Could it be bad enough not to look for survivors like me?

Staggering a step back along the house to make sure I was out of view, I felt as if I couldn't breathe, panting too hard to get the oxygen from the air. My head felt so light.

With runaway breath, I stared to the woman; just a pile of clothes I could barely see.

She didn't move as I strained to look whilst peering past the stars raining down my vision as the darkness crept in from the edges. I felt as if I would die if I couldn't control my breathing, despite what I already knew from the textbooks.

There was nothing I could do to stop my vision shrinking.

With the little control I had left, I dropped to my knees, falling most of the way before the darkness fell to leave me with what I hoped wasn't my final thought.

Would they see me?

5

With a sharp breath, light poured in, the wall's brick pattern coming into view as the brightness settled after a few moments.

I sat up, leaning to the front of the house. For a second I wondered where I was and how I got there. Then came the sound of the truck and racket of thin metal resounding with hits and the high whir of power tools.

As the memories flooded back, I tried to calm my

breath from racing away for a second time.

I decided not to look around the corner or to the body. I tried not to think of her name. I tried not to remember when I'd seen her around Cowithick so many times before. Outside the school. In the newsagents talking to Dan.

Mrs Finch. Madeline Finch. I tried not to remember her gossiping with Mum.

Screwing up my eyes, somehow I held back the scream as her face loomed in my mind with her smile looking back from around the shelves in the newsagent.

No, I told myself in silence and pressed my palms against the brick, leaning against the wall to steady myself as I rose to my feet. I held still as I let go of the wall.

Looking back in the direction of my hideout in the shop, I turned, for a fleeting moment considering peering back around the corner to see if it had really happened.

Despite knowing what I'd see, I couldn't stop myself from taking those few steps to look, pausing only when I spotted the heap on the road. But it wasn't a heap. She was a person. She was Madeline Finch.

About to turn away, a soldier at the checkpoint stepped away from the main group, rushing toward the one who'd issued the command. I heard him trying to talk but all I made out was dull noise. Nearly at his colleague, he pulled the gas mask from his face. The soldier he ran to shook his head.

Sweat poured down his bright red face as he looked between the other soldier and the woman's body. I heard everything he shouted.

"Why? We don't know if she was infected. We have to check first, then send them to quarantine. We can't just kill everyone."

The other soldier stepped toward him, slinging his rifle over his shoulder by the strap and pushed his hands out to stop the other man getting any closer. When the one without the mask continued to shake his head, the other soldier pulled off his mask, revealing his red sweating face.

"Those are not our orders, Private. Now get back to the line or I'm having your rifle."

The private pushed out his weapon for the other to take. "I'm not killing our people without a very fucking good reason."

"There's no fucking cure. If we let any one of them live, we're all fucked. You," he said, jabbing his finger at the other's chest. "Your wife and your unborn kid."

I watched, unable to turn away from the exchange as the words slowly digested in my head. As I tried to think about what he was saying, both of them turned in my direction.

Ducking out of sight, I had no idea if they'd seen me and I ran, knowing I had no other choice but to get out of the village.

With the cold road felt through the thin soles of my slippers, thoughts of escape cycled in my head. There were two ways out by car, both using the single road cutting the village in half. The blocked north entrance was where I'd run from and I could only guess the southern entrance would be the same.

But Cowithick wasn't some suburban housing estate. A handful of houses had plenty of space between them and there were many ways to get out of its circle and past the ring of meadow to the surrounding fields tall with corn in the summer.

This time of year they'd be fallow, not providing any cover if the army were patrolling. But in an area to the east, a little way from my house, an evergreen wood led out to the main road.

I knew the woods well, having played there since I could walk. We'd spent most of my childhood with friends, playing hide and seek and scaring ourselves half to death when we thought we'd got lost.

I once spent a night out there with my best friend Paul, but it was too creepy at night. Although we would never tell our parents the reason, it was the one and only time we had the courage to do so.

Noises kept us wide awake and we didn't sleep a wink.

After that we played there less and less; our enthusiasm for the place had waned and we started taking school more seriously. When we discovered games consoles, we never visited again. But through the woods you could easily get to the junction of the main road whilst staying in perfect cover.

I thought of Paul as the echo of his name died in my head, thankful he was away with his parents seeing his grandad somewhere up north for Christmas.

The woods were the place to head to, but taking the direct route meant going past my house and reliving the nightmare that started this all off.

Still running in the opposite direction of the roadblock, my nerves pulsed as a loud gunshot flashed into the air, as if I'd been shot. Tripping over my slippers, I picked up my feet when I felt no pain and the echo fell away.

Soon I regained a rhythm and with the corner of the street opening out, I saw movement, a dark figure in my path. I didn't linger to see if it was a crazed maniac or trigger-happy soldier.

Instead, diving to the left, I rushed past the short

garden gate, glaring at the handle of the front door in hope it would open if I slapped it down.

Tripping up the steps I'd only just seen, my palms grazed on the rough concrete as I held my face from the impact. I scrabbled back to my feet, still staring to the metal bar that could mean the difference between life and death. Lunging to the cold metal, the door opened as I pushed down, my foot catching on the threshold and tipping me forward, sending my knees into the rough hair and faded black letters of the coconut mat.

Ignoring the pain in my toes and the sting at my legs, I scrabbled forward. Only partway through the door, I half stood up and half crawled, tripping again as my feet left the mat, landing on the soft carpet.

With no time to savour the warmth of the thick pile, I turned, crawling on my hands and knees in hope I wouldn't be as easy to spot. Only then did I look out of the door and the direction of where I'd seen movement.

A dark figure, a man with a stilted walk, moved along the path, his gaze roving across the view as if in search of something.

I pushed the front door, forgetting how easy it had opened, tensing as it slammed hard against the frame, the noise reverberating around the house.

"Shit," I said, unable to unsay the word, immediately regretting the volume I added to my first mistake.

There would be no chance he hadn't heard. There was no chance he wasn't heading this way. I had to run. I had to get back out into the open.

As I reached up to pull on a side table beside the front door, it tipped. Spilling the phone and vase of flowers, it sent cloudy water across the carpet. When the glass didn't smash, I paused, knowing it could have been so much worse.

I rose to my feet, taking more care, then looked to the door in search of a chain, but when I saw nothing that could help, I ran along the short hallway and regretted the delay. Pushing open a door at the far end, light spilled out from the kitchen windows and glass panels of the back door.

I glanced back, catching a shadow moving across the diffused glass in the top half of the front door. I didn't want to linger, but peering across the kitchen, I looked to half-full cereal bowls sitting on the side counters and plates spread out across the surface. Toasted bread rested upright in the toaster and two mugs stood by the kettle. When I saw the long knife beside the uncut loaf on the chopping board, I stared for longer than I should.

I was afraid to give the question too much thought. Should I take the few extra steps and lean out to grab the knife? I remembered the special assemblies in school. To carry a knife was so much more dangerous than not to. But the policeman on the stage was talking about the inner cities, or the suburbs at least. Could they really have thought of this circumstance, when self-defence could mean the difference between life and death?

A dull thud along the corridor drained my enthusiasm for staying in the house any longer and I left the knife sitting on the wooden block, hoping I wouldn't regret the decision moments later.

Dropping my hand to the back door handle, I pushed down, guiding the door to swing open. Cold air rushed over me, chilling the sweat in my armpits as I ran with the short grass pushing through a hole in the sole of my slippers.

I didn't linger. A smile rose as I peered along the

length of the garden, looking to the fence standing at waist height and the strip of grass stretching out beyond, meeting the turned dirt.

A low, bass call killed my rising mood as I recognised the heavy engines of the trucks I'd seen on either side of the roadblock. Without looking, not needing to see to know what I had to do, I changed course, turning left and bounding the short fence to the garden next door.

Tripping as I landed, I then rushed to my feet and with the next fence already coming close, I regained my balance. Panting for breath, I regretted the hours on the Xbox.

I slowed, taking more care to climb over the next fence and so not to knock over the ceramic pots full of dirt, ready for planting when the weather turned. The engine noise grew to the background of the metal clatter.

I ran in brief bursts, slowing only to jump the low fences to the next garden.

On seeing a truck stationary ahead, I pulled up from a burst of speed. With its crane arm extended, soldiers in gas masks and camouflage guided hefty blocks of concrete as another stood high on the truck-bed, barking muffled instructions and sweeping his rifle across the view.

Momentum carried me forward, clattering to the fence panel as I dropped to a crouch. When a call came from a soldier, I hoped his noise had masked the bang of my body against the wood.

With heaving breath, all I could do was wait and listen to the orders I couldn't quite make out because of their face coverings.

As I peered around the garden, I knew this wasn't the place to stop. Just before I'd seen the truck as I came around the curve, I caught my first sight of the edge of the wood. Now I knew the only course of action was to go back through a house and out to the front to continue my escape.

Crouching closer to the ground, I turned to look to the back door and wished I could know by sight if it was locked, but the dark wooden frame and brass handle gave nothing away. I looked up to the windows. The top two were open, but in our close community it wasn't unusual to leave them like that when people went to work. The crime rate was non-existent. At least, it had been.

Shivering, I knew I had no choice but to take the risk. I couldn't wait crouched behind the fence to freeze to death or be spotted and shot. I had to crawl close to the ground and hope the soldier's work distracted them.

Easing through my aching joints, I lay flat to the grass whilst trying to imagine myself as a snake I'd seen so many times on nature programmes. Mum would make me watch them in a vain wish it would add context to my studies. I hoped I was close enough to the ground that they would have to look directly into the garden to notice me.

My breath steadied when I'd made it halfway with no call to bring weapons to bear and take me out.

Whilst keeping low to the grass, I angled my head up and looked along the brickwork to make sure I headed on the right course. At the sight of a camouflaged figure moving back from one of the top windows, I froze.

It wasn't the time for indecision. If there was a soldier in the house, I would open the door to my death. If there wasn't, then my neighbours would scream the house down, but at least I'd have a few moments to run through the front door and out of sight from the soldiers who would chase after me.

Or I'd seen nothing, perhaps just a reflection from the soldiers working at the edge of the field, or a figment of my racing imagination.

I pressed ahead. There was no right way. I knew I had to get anywhere other than lying flat to the grass in my pyjamas and a coat.

The grass became concrete as I edged forward, scratching at my already grazed palms and knees. Grimacing through the pain, I headed along the path towards the back door and the dark-brown wood splitting the misted glass into quarters.

I'd made my decision, the risk too much to jump another fence to try another door. If there was someone in the window and they'd seen me, then I was done for anyway, but the soldiers would be sure to see me if I stood and jumped into another garden.

As I reached the door, I slowly raised myself to a crouch, listening out for any change in the soldier's tone.

I raised my hand up whilst trying to keep as low as I could. My fingertips touched at the cold, curling around the metal just as the soldier's voice turned high-pitched.

A muffled shout called out, followed by a barrage of gunfire and the clattering of falling metal as I pulled down at the handle.

It didn't move. I was toast.

6

Without conscious thought, instinct took over. My hand dropped to my side, my eyes screwing closed as I wrapped my hands to grip my ankles, clenching in some primal urge to make myself as small as possible.

The shots kept coming, my body shaking with each round and I couldn't help thinking it wouldn't be much longer before they would hit.

What would the impact be like? Would I feel pain straight away or would it take my body a few seconds to realise it was being ripped wide? Or perhaps I'd never know. Would I be grateful if a bullet hit me right in the brain and I went out like a light? At least it would be an end to the nightmare.

When a touch came at my upper arm, I nearly didn't react. I was so prepared for it all to end, I couldn't help the surprise that my first thought had been right. The bullet felt as if someone had touched my arm. Not a searing pain but a sudden pressure. A pull towards the door.

But that couldn't be right.

As I fell forward, past where the door should have been, I opened my eyes with my arms still wrapping me up. I looked up and saw a kid; a boy of maybe half my age, dressed in green and black pyjamas with a plastic dark helmet and the words MP in white across the front.

Blinking to make sure I was seeing right, I turned back to the garden as I rose and took a step, half pulled by the kid. Each of the soldiers in the distance had their weapons raised, puffs of smoke coming with each loud noise, but they pointed to where I'd wanted to be and not in my direction.

I fell to the kitchen floor as the kid let go and he rushed past me to push the door closed. He stood with his back to the glass, staring at me as I sprawled to the floor.

"Jordan?" he asked, his eyes lighting up.

"Tommy," I said, nodding as I realised I must have

been in number fifty-four; ten houses down from mine.

He smiled with a wide grin.

"Where are your parents?" I said, but before he could answer, I stood, grabbing his hand so I could draw him to the floor. "Keep down."

He looked back, the grin gone and for the first time I saw the uncertainty in his face as his body juddered every time another shot came. I put my hand to his cheek and looked him in the eyes whilst trying not to blink with each new burst of noise.

"It's just like fireworks," I said.

His lips raised a little again and I imagined him thinking of a black night, his face glowing from the huge bonfire and the multi-colours mirrored in his eyes as the rockets shot to the sky.

The gunfire stopped.

"Where are your parents?" I said again.

He shook his head and I pulled my hand away when his high voice cracked as he spoke. "Dad's at work and Mum went out to the shop but she didn't come back. That was hours ago."

"It's okay," I said, the first words that came into my head even though everything I'd seen made me think the opposite.

"Why are those soldiers putting up a fence around the village?" he said, and for a moment I thought about the question. Why was that the first question he asked and not why those soldiers were shooting at people?

But then I realised what he'd said. I'd been right. That is what they were trying to do. "Can you see from upstairs?" I said.

Tommy nodded, looking behind me.

Crawling along the floor, I checked back to make sure he followed. Reaching the hallway, I rose to my feet, bounding up the stairs. At first I ran to the left and a room looking out on the back garden. I didn't rush right up to the window; instead, I held my arms wide at my sides so Tommy wouldn't either. Taking slow steps, I stood as far back as I could from the net curtains covering the glass, stopping when I had an unobstructed view.

The soldiers were building a wall around the village to stop anyone getting out. They didn't think there were survivors and weren't giving anyone a chance to tell them otherwise. Soon there would be no getting out and they'd condemn everyone inside.

But not me. They wouldn't keep me trapped, but I had to do something before they finished encircling the village. I had to make a run for it.

The fence had already lengthened towards the house so quickly in the past few minutes and I jumped at the sight of something moving to the right, calming when I saw it was another lorry dropping off more panels. Two masked soldiers stood on the back and scanned the view with the muzzles of their rifles raised.

I turned, beckoning for Tommy to follow, and as I did, I looked along the fence to the left. It stretched out as far as I could see. I would have to be quick to get to the woods before they blocked us in. If that happened, I knew we wouldn't last much longer.

Running out of the room, I noticed for the first time Tommy still stood in his camouflage pyjamas. "Get dressed. Keep away from the window. Make sure you grab some shoes," I said.

He looked at me, holding there for a second before peering down to my ragged slippers. "My dad's shoes might fit you."

Pausing for a moment, I thought on his words,

nodding when I realised what he'd said and how much I wanted to get something more substantial on my feet. I looked back, watching him frown.

"What?" I said when he hadn't voiced the question I could tell he was desperate to ask.

"Shall I brush my teeth?"

I couldn't help but smile at his innocence and I nodded, watching him rush to the bathroom and something dawned on me. Shit. I would have to look after him.

Perhaps it might be better to stay in the house and push the furniture in front of the doors, then just wait for them to find out there were survivors who weren't crazed with the infection.

I looked around the bedroom at the big furniture, thinking how I could push the wardrobe down the stairs so no one would stand a chance of moving it from the other side of the door. Tommy rushed back into the room with his toothbrush in his hand and his lips pouting.

"There's no water in the tap."

"Shit," I said, watching as his brow relaxed and he smiled with his eyes wide. "Sorry. I shouldn't swear."

Tommy shook his head, still smiling. With no water, we couldn't stay in the house.

Rushing across the hallway into what I guessed would have been his parents' room, the double bed stripped of its dressing with the duvet and pillows bare, I approached the window and its view out of the opposite side of the house. Despite my caution, I let myself get nearer this time, waiting for my eyes to adjust through the net curtains.

To the right, I saw my house. I saw Steve's car and the Ford Focus still to its side. I had a clear view of where

Steve had crouched on top of the guy and half expected a body to be in the road, but in its place was a dark patch as if someone had thrown a bucket of water to wash away the blood.

Unless the darkness was the blood.

I looked up toward the other road and the houses in the middle, sandwiched between those forming the ring around the village. I saw over most of them and apart from where the newsagent, the pub and the church blocked the view in the middle, it was easy to see the road cutting the village in two. It was easier still to see the fence almost complete on the far side.

They were trying to keep us in. I had no doubt, but where were all the neighbours? Where were the rest of the village?

Footsteps from behind made me turn and I saw Tommy closing the door of his room. I twisted back as movement in the corner of my eyes came from near my house. A figure walked past, but not on the pavement. They were right up to the brickwork. In the short front garden, they were walking strangely, like people did when they'd had way too much to drink.

A shot rang out through the air and I flinched away from the window, forcing my eyes closed.

When I opened them as the echo died, the figure lay on the grass with a new dark mark staining the brickwork of my house.

More movement pulled my attention to the left and I watched a line of soldiers marching up the street in a loose formation, each in gas masks, moving to stand by a front door. With a heavy thud and a shout, I watched them throw something inside and jerk back flat to the walls.

A loud explosion sent me for ducking for cover.

7

"What was that?" Tommy said in his high voice, having changed into jeans and a hoodie. I shook my head, leaning back to the window and looking to where the soldiers had been only moments before, but all I saw was the last of them disappearing through the door they'd just thrown a grenade into.

I watched, only able to pull away when bursts of gunshots started. They were clearing the houses.

Stumbling from the window, I turned to Tommy.

"We've got to go."

Ushering him down the stairs, about to put my hand on the door, I looked at him.

"Where are your dad's shoes?" I asked, watching as he pointed along the short hallway and the cupboard under the stairs.

Pulling the cupboard open, I hurried the worn slippers from my feet, but the two pairs I tried were far too small for my size tens. When I felt another explosion through the wall, I gave up, pushing my slippers back on.

Before I opened the door, I grabbed Tommy's wrist, then peered left to glimpse soldiers rushing into the next house with smoke still pouring from the front door. It was a scene I would have expected to see on the TV news of some conflict in a third-world country.

It was worse than I thought. They were going from house to house to make sure there was no one left alive. They weren't even checking if people were acting weird. I'd heard no calls to check if the people in the house were afflicted. The soldiers were killing people on sight.

What had the world come to? Was whatever had affected my mum, Steve and everyone else I'd seen in the village so far so dangerous? Was there no way they could get better? Was there no hope for me, or Tommy?

It was like a video game; like the one I'd been playing that morning, but at least then I'd had a gun. Perhaps if I could get one, it would even up our odds.

I pictured a soldier lying dead, attacked by someone from the village and bleeding out by the side of the road. Could I take the rifle from his body?

Dismissing the thought with a shake of my head and about to turn to Tommy, I stopped, seeing movement from over the road. A door opened two houses along and an Asian man in boxer shorts with a woman in a dressing gown behind him stepped over the threshold. Both looked around in search of what was going on.

I recognised their faces but not their names. I'd seen them before, like everyone else in Cowithick.

The muffled commands from the soldiers pulled me away from the question of their name, the calls growing more frantic. I imagined them shouting for them to stay where they were and get to their knees, but they wouldn't do as they were told.

As if in a daze, they looked on as the soldiers ran toward them with their rifles raised.

Still stood in the doorway, I wanted to call out. I wanted to tell them to turn and run, bar the door and rush out of the back like I needed to do. But I couldn't get the words out.

Seeing the soldiers hadn't looked my way, I stepped back into the house, closing the door but leaving just a crack so I could peer out. I watched the inevitable gun shot, the first of many cutting the man down, sending him stumbling back with a look of utter shock as he clutched his chest.

The woman screamed, dropping to her knees, then

turned back to their doorway where a kid stood with his mouth wide.

Mo. I knew his name. He was only a year younger than me.

His mum tried to stand, but a plume of blood sprayed backward before she could rise. I turned away, gripping Tommy's head as the volley of explosions came, bucking my body with each echo between the houses.

As the gunfire halted, I released Tommy, keeping my body between him and the terrible sight I couldn't bring myself to look at. I looked past the first sign of his tears and gripped him by the upper arms.

"We have to run," I said.

By his slow nod, he understood, but from his hardened expression I couldn't tell if he'd seen the result of the shots fired. I couldn't tell if he realised the soldiers weren't there to reunite him with his mother.

He didn't give any other reply, and I gripped hard, releasing my hold just a little when he tensed as if in pain.

"Do you understand that we have to get away?"

He nodded.

"I know somewhere I think will be safe. Somewhere where we can look for your dad." I nodded, hoping to prompt the same again in return.

His reply was much shallower, but his eyes lit up when I spoke again.

"So when we hear that loud noise again, we have to run. Hold my hand and go as fast as you can. Do you understand?"

He nodded and I forced a smile as he mirrored my expression. The only difference was that mine fell as soon as he couldn't see. I leaned to the wall to wait whilst holding my hand out toward him at my back.

His hand felt so small in mine. I was sixteen and

closer to being a fully-grown adult, whereas he had such a long way to go. So much of his life to live.

They hadn't even bothered to move the bodies. Edging forward, I saw the soldiers had moved back to the house they'd been at before the man had stepped out. I ducked back when I thought I saw a soldier glance my way, holding my breath until I heard the call and I knew what would come next.

"Get ready," I said, tensing.

Boom.

The pressure wave rattled the windows and I ran, hunched over, out of the door with my arm trailing behind me as I dragged Tommy from the house. He kept up and I didn't glance left, instead aiming straight for the front garden gate, still wide open.

We were out so quickly, slowing only enough for the turn right, then speeding again as I gripped Tommy tight. Together we rushed to get around the path's curve and put us out of sight of the soldiers before they left the house they'd rushed into just after the explosion.

I soon saw my house and I kept running, but slowing just a little to put myself between Tommy and the house in hope he wouldn't see the corpse crumpled in our front garden.

I looked to the cars still embedded in each other, the mark where my brother had fought the stranger. Strange, because I hadn't seen him before Steve had attacked.

The dark mark hadn't been water and I was glad when it went out of sight as we came level with the house.

With Tommy's pull on my hand, I glanced back, but I couldn't see the soldiers. The optimism soon fell away when another blast filled the air, chased by a single gunshot.

I sped, but had to slow when Tommy couldn't keep up.

Above the tops of the houses opposite, I saw the first signs of the trees rising higher than the roofs. With adrenaline rushing and a desperation to pick Tommy up and run faster, I slowed at the sight of my friend's house and their little white Ford in the driveway. The front door of the house stood wide with what looked like blood splattered up the cream walls inside.

They must have come home from their trip early.

What choice did I have other than to run to the building splattered in blood where my best friend could lie dead or maimed by someone caught up with the madness? Or where he could be alive?

If I raced in would there still be someone inside who would attack me? What would I do with Tommy? The soldiers were on their way and I already knew they wouldn't hold back their explosives and guns for someone my age. I didn't want to test if they would for someone of Tommy's.

But could I run past his house and risk leaving my friend to die?

Glancing back, I still couldn't see soldiers around the curve, but I heard what sounded like the hammering of something heavy against wood, taking me back to the many police programmes I loved to watch and the Big Red Key the police used to knock down front doors.

But that was all about crime, drugs or wanted people, not breaking into their homes to kill them in case a disease from the water or in the air had overcome them.

If I was well and I felt fine, Tommy too, then there would be other people. Cowithick had a population of around three hundred. The same fate couldn't have overcome them all. I just couldn't believe we were the only two left.

Rushing across the road, still holding Tommy's hand, I glanced to the right to make sure we didn't put ourselves in the sight of the soldiers making their way toward us. Avoiding the view of the blood along the white of the wall, I couldn't help but stare at the trail as it climbed the single step to lead to the dark carpet inside.

My stomach tightened and it felt as if my breakfast would empty to join the blood. I tried to lift my legs and rise to enter the house.

I couldn't bring myself to. Instead, and to the sound of hammering at a stubborn door down the road, I called out with the paltry amount of breath I dared to spend.

"Paul?"

The sound came out so light and I tried again, but it wouldn't rise any louder. I felt so afraid of everything around me and I just wanted to run.

I closed my eyes, trying to build up the courage to call out again, this time with volume.

His name stopped halfway when I saw a Nike Air trainer with a foot inside on the floor at the end of the hall, the ankle leading out of sight.

I knew it was Paul's trainer and when I heard a noise coming from inside the house, I could do nothing more than turn and run away, dragging Tommy behind.

As I ran, the guilt made me feel so heavy and the thoughts pulled me down. I couldn't help but think I'd not seen what I thought I had. Perhaps someone had borrowed Paul's shoes and the noise was from him trying to signal me.

Already regretting not going into the house to check, I knew it was too late. If it wasn't him on the floor, then I'd sealed his fate. I could have been his last chance, but I was running off to save myself and Tommy.

Between the next house and the one after that, a significant gap of grass waited with a dirt track beyond. It was one of the many routes dog walkers would take to get to the woods or the green belt surrounding the village.

As we arrived, we headed down between the houses, but I pulled up sharply, coming to a stop when I saw the normal view of the ploughed fields or rising corn was blocked with a line of battered metal fence panels. Looking closer, in the small gap between each I saw the large square lumps coming up to waist height to weigh down each support on the other side.

8

I shuffled forward, looking left and right, letting go of Tommy's hand with a quick glance to make sure he still followed.

I looked over every surface of the fence, wondering if I could scale it whilst wishing they'd put the concrete blocks on this side to make it easier.

I glanced to Tommy and he looked back, his brow raised with a question. Maybe I could have climbed over, but I wasn't sure if Tommy would have the strength even if I boosted him up.

At the edge of the back of the house and about to come out of the safety of the brick cover on either side, I looked both ways along the gardens and down the gap between the fence and the end of each of the small plots of land. With no new danger, I turned, whispering for Tommy to wait.

I hunched over, stepping lightly before rushing to the end of the garden.

Glancing to either side and seeing nothing to hold me back, I moved up to the panels which seemed so much taller up close. I couldn't even reach the top, despite being nearly six foot. I was a long way off being able to grab at the edge.

Shaking my head and with hope fading, I looked down to a finger-width gap between the metal and the grass.

I touched at the metal, pushing against the cold with the palm of my hand. The panel moved away, then stopped as it hit against the concrete block on the other side. I leaned in with my shoulder, pushing with all my weight, but it held firm.

On the edge of tears, I felt a movement behind me. Spinning around, panicking when I couldn't see Tommy waiting between the houses, there he was at my side with his shoulder pushing against the fence.

His gesture seemed to warm me a little inside. I stopped pushing and shook my head at him, forcing a smile as he stood upright.

"We'll find another way," I said in a whisper, watching as he nodded, blinking rapidly.

I thought about getting a car and ramming it through, questioning if it would even work. Looking back on the path we'd taken, there would be no chance of getting a car between the houses. But there were other places I could try, although I couldn't remember if there were any that would break out close to the woods. And all this without being spotted by the soldiers.

With my hand still against the panel, an explosion rang out in the air, the pressure rumbling through the metal. Pulling my hand away, I looked down to Tommy peering up, his pale face mirroring my panic. Then his expression changed as the echo died. Ignoring the calls in the background, he raised his hand, grabbing mine from my side and gripping hard.

Nodding, I tried to take on his hope, despite the deep sounds coming from all around. The clatter of panels. The distance calls. Heavy boots against the tarmac. An explosion and occasional gunshot. Each sound amplified by the fence and reflected into the village.

My mind wandered to the sound wave experiments we'd done with string at school, followed by a rush of panic that I still hadn't started revision.

I thought of the school. I had another week off until the end of the holidays but then I realised I may never have a normal life again. Or a life at all if I didn't get my act together.

Despite the growing feeling of helplessness as I looked along the row of gardens, each empty beyond their low fences, I peered down the alley I'd come through. Looking that way and with a lull to the noise, there was nothing to show what was happening all around us.

A scream cried out, breaking my trance, the call echoing in the distance, leaving me feeling so exposed in the open space. A new panicked cry came, deeper than a woman could make, but the voice was soon replaced with the rush of feet. An explosion followed, sounding so close, then the shatter of glass. I took hope there must be other people who had survived, although I knew each moment that passed their number would shrink.

I couldn't think about them; I had to worry about myself and Tommy.

Still staring out between the houses, my heart sank

as with a heavy engine sound, what looked like a small tank drove across the narrow view.

Looking down to Tommy, his limp smile told me he'd seen it too. I turned away, the need to find a way out of the village growing with every moment.

Gripping Tommy's hand tight, we ran along the backs of the gardens, the short fences at the end of the gardens to our left and the tall metal fence always present to our right. With each step I looked to the back of the houses, hurriedly searching for anything of use; something to help us climb or somehow get through the metal.

I peered to the sheds of all sizes, each with their doors shut up and a heavy padlock across the front. I imagined the tools inside, thinking back to the collection of junk my dad built up before he died; a collection Mum still hadn't been able to throw away, despite Dad being gone for three years.

His memory forced my legs to slow as I tried to push away the thought of how things would have been different if he was still around. He would have taken charge. Dad would have known what to do without question. He would have kept Steve and Mum safe and would have told me exactly how to act.

But he wasn't around and I had no choice but to shake away the thoughts, pushing down the anger that he was taken away so early in my life. Instead, I concentrated on looking around the curve of the houses, slowing when I knew we were getting near to where the semi-circle met the other end of the road out of the village.

Seeing scaffolding wrapped around the back of a house, I stopped. The Jamesons' place. They were having their roof redone. I remembered the news relayed by

Mum a few days ago, the perfect example of the level of excitement I'd give anything to get back to.

But there it was, a ladder fixed to the inside of the scaffolding and exactly what I needed to get us to the safety of the woods, if it hadn't been bolted down.

9

A new metallic drumming sound called into the silence. Half expecting to see a soldier checking their handiwork with a slap of the hand, I ducked down, guiding Tommy with me as I looked along the line of gardens.

When it wasn't a camouflaged figure in a gas mask I saw but a man in a dark business suit and red shirt who looked like Mr Jackson, the bank manager from a few doors down, I almost stood up again. He'd come into view along the fence-line, picking himself up from the grass as if he'd fallen into the metal panel.

"There," Tommy called before I thought to keep him quiet.

The man looked in our direction. With his hands limp by his sides, I was sure it was Mr Jackson heading our way.

Elation rose as he drew closer and I stood when every step reassured me it was the man my parents had introduced me to. Someone like him would know what to do. He'd know how to get us out of this mess.

Still without hurrying, he headed our way. I wanted to call out and make him rush, not knowing how long it would be before the soldiers found us. But he remained calm, pushing one foot in front the other as if his legs hurt.

My smile grew at his composure, but as he drew

closer, I realised what I thought was a red shirt was actually an apron of blood around his neck.

Before I could look any more, he tripped, on what I couldn't see, but he fell to the grass. As he rose, a great flap of skin hung from the back of his neck, slapping against raw flesh as he tried to get to his feet.

"What the hell?" I said, then gripping tight to Tommy's hand I turned, pulling him along until his little legs caught up. I didn't look back, running the way we'd come whilst glancing to each of the gardens as we rushed past.

We ran to the sound of Tommy's questions, slowing only as we passed the place where we'd come between the houses. We jogged a short while for Tommy to catch his breath.

Then I saw it. A gap between the houses I'd not noticed before; a gap wide enough to get a car through to smash out the fence metal and get to safety.

Fighting to fill my lungs, and despite not knowing how to drive, the car seemed like the best option now. All I had to do was find one, get into it, work out how to drive and do it all without being attacked by the crazed villagers or shot by the soldiers.

But what else could I do?

Energised by the quickly forming plan, and with a glance back to make sure we'd left Mr Jackson far behind, I ran between the houses. Dragging Tommy along, I stopped only as we came to the edge of the brickwork.

I peered to either side, reminding myself where in the street we'd emerged. Not seeing any movement along the road or at any of the houses, I turned my attention to the parked cars. There were a lot to choose from.

Looking back to the fence, I tried to visualise the

biggest car that would fit between the giant blocks.

Turning around, I crept forward, mindful to check on either side before focusing on each of the driveways.

I wasn't big into cars, probably because my dad hadn't been. He'd had a BMW when he'd died, but we got rid of that. My mum had a small runabout to get to work and do the shopping in. It was affordable, she said, and easy to drive. We didn't need anything fancy.

Almost half of the cars were similar to Mum's Ford, but although the smaller cars would be simpler, I couldn't decide if they would have enough power and weight to get me through the fence. A smile raised on my lips as an equation from my textbooks came into my head; force equals mass times acceleration. The bigger the car and the faster it travelled, the more likely we would be to bust through the metal, snapping the links between the panels so we could race to the woods.

The smile stayed when I wondered if my physics teacher ever had that use in mind.

If only I knew the weight of the car, perhaps I could do the calculation to save my life and revise at the same time.

I laughed, looking down to Tommy as he peered up. He frowned back as if wondering if the stress had sent me round the twist.

Shaking my head to brush away his concern, I looked back at the cars in search of the biggest. If I could master the controls, perhaps I wouldn't need to stop at the woods, instead driving straight across the fields to the main road.

Admiring a red four by four gleaming on the drive a few doors down, memories from a few months ago flooded back; Mum telling me how excited the Williams were to get their new car. I felt the press of guilt, but with it came a tinge of wickedness and excitement at the thought of taking their brand-new car and smashing it through the fence.

I just had to get the keys and figure out how to drive before the soldiers came to take the place apart.

I'd made my mind up, but the front door was closed. About to tell Tommy to wait as I tried the handle, I heard an engine to the right.

There was a tall green truck coming around the curve of the street with six or more soldiers running alongside.

Freezing to the spot, we watched as they stopped and pushed open the gate of the nearest house. Knowing what would come next, I turned, guiding Tommy back between the houses.

After counting along the row, we stood at the short wooden fence outside the rear of the William's place. The tidy garden was mostly grass, much like the front. I looked to the shed, its door locked with a large padlock. Beside it stood a light-green storage container. In the centre of the grass was a round pond with a nozzle rising in the middle, but the pump was quiet with no water spraying out to splash the large rocks.

The handle at the back door didn't move as I pushed down. I had no idea if it meant the Williams were safe and sound inside, oblivious to what had happened this morning. How could anyone have missed the chaos, the sirens, gunshots or explosions?

I hoped instead they'd gone away on holiday, perhaps not wanting to leave their shiny new car at the airport. Or had they already run out to the madness, locking the door behind them?

Either way, if I wanted the car on their drive, I would have to find out. A distant explosion echoed from the other side of the house.

There was no sign of movement beyond the blinds over the kitchen window or the curtains across the rest. The frosted glass in the top half of the back door would only let me see the light coming from the front.

"Go hide by that box," I whispered to Tommy as I crouched.

He looked back, his eyes wide with alarm.

"It's okay," I said, forcing a smile as I pulled a Kit Kat from my pocket. His expression relaxed and he took the chocolate before turning to run between the shed and storage box. Grimacing at whatever I couldn't see, after a pause he crouched, leaving only his round face and mop of hair in view.

Turning away, I hoped I wouldn't regret not bringing him with me.

With a step to the water feature, I took a smooth grey rock the size of my fist and headed back to the door. Giving a gentle tap at the frosted glass, I cringed at the sound, edging back as I waited for something to happen. I wasn't sure if I paused for the glass to shatter or for someone from the village to charge out from nowhere and attack.

Either way, nothing happened and I stepped back up to the door, raising the rock a second time.

Checking again beyond the frosted glass, I reassured myself I'd seen no movement. They must have been on holiday and taken a taxi to the airport, spending Christmas and New Year somewhere hot, or somewhere cold. Skiing perhaps?

The Williams had two children. A girl and a boy, both a few years younger than me. Young enough that I barely spoke to either of them, especially as they went to the posh school half an hour away.

Posh school. They must be skiing. I tapped the window with the rock, harder this time, letting go as it went through the pane, sending glass shattering to the floor.

Pulling my hand back, I held my breath as I waited for anything to react to the terrible sound.

10

When no shadows moved across the other side of the front door, I looked back to Tommy who'd raised his head and peered at the missing glass. I stared to Tommy for a moment longer until he ducked down below the cover. I turned back to the door just as the remaining shard slipped from the frame, shattering to the floor.

Despite the fear of who could be the other side, I knew I had little time to worry. What could be worse than doing nothing? What could be worse than being found hiding by a soldier and shot without explanation, or attacked by one of my neighbours?

Whilst focusing on the razor-sharp fragments still in the frame, I peered in and then pushed my hand through the missing pane, hoping for a key sitting in the lock.

It was empty. I turned, rushing over to Tommy who was still wide-eyed and glancing between me and the missing window, seeming to question what I was doing.

Grabbing one of the large potting boxes by his side, I bounded back over to the door. With the boom of an explosion not so far away, I stood on the upturned box to give me a little more height. Taking care to avoid the remaining glass, I edged foot first through the space.

Dropping to the floor on the other side, I grabbed at the breakfast bar as I slid on glass with the sharp edges stinging the sole of my right foot through the thin slippers.

Shit.

Looking down as I gained my balance, I was ready to see the floor covered with my blood. When there was nothing but the many shapes of glass, I breathed a sigh of relief.

Holding myself steady against the counter, I took a deep breath, not ready to move my feet, not ready to pick out a spot on the tiles where I couldn't see the shine of light from the glass.

A few breaths later and with muffled voices heard from the front of the house, perhaps only a few doors along, I remembered why I'd taken such a risk. I had to get the car key.

But where could it be?

With a wetness at my right foot, I lifted my leg. Blood spread across the thin sole of the slipper, concentrating around a slit the width of my thumb.

The deep voices seemed so close and did nothing to ease my panic. There was nothing else I could do but grit my teeth and take the steps, tentatively placing my foot to the floor and waiting for the next sharp dig. When none came, I glanced to where I'd lifted my foot, glaring at the red circular print left behind.

I gained confidence in my steps, reminding myself to seek out the keys whilst looking anywhere but the trail I left in my wake. Relief came as I moved along the short hallway lined with plush carpet. Walking through the unfamiliar layout, I peered to the front door where, if we'd lived here, Mum would have kept the keys to her tiny car on a table at its side.

There was no table.

To the right under the stairs was a small door and as I opened it, I stopped midway when the hinges gave a low creak, leaving the door open enough to see there wasn't a cupboard full of coats and shoes as I'd expected. Instead, a toilet sat on a white-tiled floor with a sink in the corner.

I shut the door.

To the left, I guessed the next door would take me to a living room or lounge, but as each of the houses in Cowithick were so different, I couldn't be sure until I built up the courage to look.

The pain from my foot grew with every step, but I pushed on, opening the door to two wide sofas arranged in front of a huge TV in the corner. There were no decorations of the season, confirming the Williams were definitely away.

As I stepped in, another explosive boom stopped my search as I felt the sound through the floor. I spotted a set of car keys resting on a side table beside a stack of round coasters. My stomach flipped at the sight, but the excitement fell away when I saw there were no front door keys on the ring.

Looking up to the wide window, a shadow moved beyond the net curtains. Two soldiers were taking considered steps along the pavement just past the front garden. They were coming to break open the door and throw in their grenade with no questions asked.

I peered on as the black gas mask of the lead soldier looked my way, as if he'd seen me beyond the thin netted material.

Ducking down as far as I could, I leapt towards the keys, trying to stay low whilst gritting my teeth as pain stung my foot.

I swiped the key fob from the table, knocking the coasters to the floor. Rising as I reached the hallway, through the needles of pain, I rushed out into the corridor. Shaking my head, I looked left to the dark figures through the misted glass, hoping they hadn't seen me blocking out their light.

When they hadn't opened fire, I retraced my bloodied prints to the back of the house.

Bang came the big red ram at the front as their bulk blotted out the light. When at the kitchen door a sudden pain shot up from my right heel, my ankle collapsed, sending my hands out in front to stop myself from smashing my head against the door jamb.

Rushing to get to my feet, I looked to the blood dotting the kitchen floor, grimacing at the glass strewn where I knew I had to climb again. But what choice did I have?

With a second pounding at the front door, I grabbed a chair from the table to the right and dropped it to the floor amongst the glass. The heavy hits at the door hid my clumsy hand with the chair. Not slowing, knowing their effort behind me would soon be over, I had to be out of sight, hoping they'd not see the blood or the glass missing from the back door and the chair at the empty window.

I jumped through the window opening, using my hands on the frame to propel myself through the gap. Clenching my jaw to stifle any sound, I landed on my feet. It felt as if the skin had come away as I pressed down on the bare flesh underneath.

Tommy stared my way, not hiding the mixture of concern and pleasure at seeing me again.

He rose and I shook my head, waving for him to get back down as I fell to my knees, crawling back toward the house. Leaning to the brick beside the back door, I pushed myself as close to the patio slabs as I could, just in time for the explosion shocking through the ground and spraying glass out from every window.

11

I waited, shivering, expecting the soldiers to follow my bloody mess and smash down the back door. I'd turn and see them, watching as they spotted Tommy standing, gawking back and not hesitating to put a bullet between his eyes before they turned on me.

But no. I heard the shouts from behind the masks, but not the question in their voices or the sudden hush, as if they'd seen something to raise their interest. What had they already seen to make my blood on the floor pale into the background?

With a rush of boots, their deep, incoherent voices vibrated through the house. I pictured the men focused on clearing every room until their noise was no more, their absence confirmed moment later with a swift bang at the next door along, followed by a more distant explosion.

As the echo died, the pain in my foot came into focus and twisting as quickly as I dared, I turned, hoping Tommy would be where I'd left him waiting, safe and well.

But he wasn't.

I crawled from the slabs, glancing left and right, guiding myself around the glass shards littering the grass, looking to every nook for a foot, his small hands, anything as a sign of where he waited and that he hadn't run off into the sight of the soldiers.

Edging closer to the shed where I'd left him, there wasn't much more space for him to hide in. I peered forward as I crawled with my hands on the grass, when a sharp sting rose from my left hand. I pulled away, clenching my teeth and saw a shard the size of a cookie sticking out from the ground.

I looked at my hand and a cut the diameter of a coin, surprised to see no blood pouring out.

A little light-headed, I scanned the grass for more shards, then looked to my palm and the blood rolling slowly down to my wrist. My thoughts turned to my mum helping me to wash it under the sink, then dabbing it dry with such care. But I knew Mum would never make it all better again.

I was on my own.

With a tear rolling down my cheek, I felt so lost and helpless, but then I heard my name called from just ahead. There was Tommy on the edge of tears, emerging from the gap between the shed and the planter boxes.

"Tommy," I said, seeing him safe and well and staring at my hand with his eyes so wide I thought he'd split open his head. "I'm okay. It's just a little cut," I said, getting to my feet, then stumbling forward with blood dripping to the grass as I regained my balance. My foot reminded me of its damage.

"Does it hurt?" he replied.

"Just a little," I said and he nodded quickly as if he knew it wasn't true, but he wanted to believe I was okay and everything would be fine.

"I just need to find something to stop the bleeding," I said, pulling air as I tried flexing my hand, the blood quickening. I looked away, peering to the door I'd only just come out of. Being careful where I placed my feet, I headed back to the house.

A boom of pressure radiated from down the road, but quieter than the one from next door. The soldiers were making progress. Two gunshots cracked through the air and I ducked, even though I guessed they were two doors away. A flurry of incoherent voices shouted out; this was different and I couldn't help but wonder what could have caught their interest.

I couldn't let the noise slow me. I was at the back door, surprised it was still on its hinges. Peering in, I half expected to see a great crater in the centre of the hallway. But there was none. Instead, scorch marks centred around jagged metal buried in the plaster and across the wooden floor, with splinters everywhere. Smoke rose from the red embers in amongst the debris, the air heavy with chemicals.

The walls had taken the worst hit, great holes in the plaster with dust still settling. The walls on either side were ruined, but other than potted with dark marks, they were mostly intact. The toilet door seemed to have survived with only scorch marks.

I looked around to the breakfast bar and saw the tea-towel resting on the side next to the knife block. I hoped I could just about reach it, despite only able to use one hand pain free.

Leaning in through the missing pane, I pushed my arm out, wincing as I opened my hand and grabbed the towel.

Pulling the cloth through the opening, I stepped back and Tommy helped as best as he could, wrapping the towel around my palm.

To the continued soundtrack of explosions, I took a moment to regain my thoughts. A moment to remember the plan and think how I would make it around the houses and out to the front to start the car so we could make our escape through the fence. Then I remembered the key I'd held in my hand.

I searched at my feet, looking to the paving slabs spotted with my blood and then to the grass, but I couldn't see the rectangle of black plastic anywhere, the grass too short for it to be hiding there.

"No," I said, as I realised I must have dropped it inside and it would have been destroyed in the explosion. I sank to the cold of the slabs and pushed my uninjured hand to my eyes.

How could I have been so careless to drop the key inside the house?

But now wasn't the time to relent with the soldiers only a few houses away and Mr Jackson probably catching up with us at any moment. If I took too long to act, one way or another we'd die.

Tommy wrapped his arms around my head. At first I protested, but he felt so warm, his small body such a comfort. As his grip tightened, I relaxed.

A rapid burst of gunfire rattled us both and he held on as if his grip would save us. I imagined a crowd of my neighbours facing the soldiers, the guns firing before they knew what was going on.

Screams told of their pain until the echo fell away, leaving nothing behind.

I had to do something. If not for me, for Tommy. I had to do something before I could no longer keep him safe.

Unpicking myself from his grip, I took slow steps to the door. Tommy picked up the planter box from where the explosion forced it towards the pond and set it back as a stool at the foot of the door.

Looking through the missing glass, I saw its battered and disjointed panels scuffed with red paint, but at least it meant we could walk right through the house and out to the car.

Turning away, I spotted the key lying amongst the debris, but covered in dust I couldn't tell if it was still intact. There was only one way to find out. All I had to do to get us to safety was to get through the back door again, being more careful with the glass.

I stepped up on the planter box, gripping tight to the door frame as I held my feet firm, my foot staying in place despite the blood. Perhaps it was a good sign, the wound clotting. I raised a brow as an illustration of a wound from my biology textbook flashed before my eyes.

Shaking away the image and holding my injured hand to my chest, I straddled the frame again. With surprise, I found the chair still on the other side, albeit distorted and covered in plaster fragments.

Stepping to its fabric surface, I scanned the floor for glass, but the spread of debris made it almost impossible to see.

With a light touch at first, I pressed my uninjured foot to the floor. Sweeping it to the side to clear a space, I stepped down the rest of the way.

The chemical smell was so much heavier inside, along with the same smell from my brother this morning.

Tommy screwed up his face as he vaulted through the missing window with ease, glass crunching under his feet as he moved to my side and stared through the doorway to the car just beyond.

"Be careful," I whispered, but it would have been too late to make a difference.

I took a step forward, expecting any moment for the light coming through the front door to disappear as soldiers stepped out, pointing their guns and taking the two shots to finish our chances. But as we stood for what seemed like a long moment, nothing happened.

I looked to Tommy, his face seeming to shine with hope. I took a step forward, sweeping the debris aside.

With a few more steps, we were nearing the key and halfway to the front door.

Tommy sped forward, kneeling down, plucking it from the rubble, beaming back with the fob raised in his hand and a proud smile.

Five or six steps and we'd be outside. So much closer to safety.

Walking forward, my heart sank, turning to the right to the sound of the toilet flushing under the stairs.

12

I had no chance to decide what to do. I had no choice to turn and run and grab Tommy by the arm to rush back into the kitchen and dive out through the window and back to the cold ground. I had no chance to do any of those things before a red-faced man in camouflage clothes and helmet gawked back with his mouth hanging wide as both his hands fastened a thick green belt.

Seeing the rifle resting against the sink, with one step it would be in reach. I could grab it and shoot him before he could do what I knew he would to both of us. But no, there was no chance and he let go of his belt, his hands reaching to the pistol holstered at his thigh.

I wanted to turn to Tommy. I wanted to reassure him everything would be okay. The end would be quick. But Tommy was already in view, surging forward with a fierce, scrunched up expression as he charged the soldier. I followed his lead without thought and pushed out my hands, aiming for his chest, ignoring the false weight of the wound. It was that or lie down and die.

Tommy made contact first, forcing the soldier's hands away before he reached the pistol.

My hands connected, pain blooming from my palm.

The soldier stumbled back, his foot catching on the toilet, and he fell between the bowl and the wall. Wedging in the space, with one hand he tried to push Tommy away whilst fumbling for his pistol with the other.

Tommy bit down on the soldier's fingers as they lurched out. As Tommy released, the soldier pulled both his hands back, his right coming away from the clip holding the pistol tight in the holster.

Taking the chance, I had the gun in my hands, the soldier cursing, spit coming from his mouth as he shouted for the weapon back.

Grabbing Tommy by the shoulder, I pulled him backwards, my hands shaking as I pointed the pistol to the soldier's face. I watched the colour drain from his skin. His eyes were wide as I guessed he tried to figure out if I had the balls to pull the trigger.

Colour came back to his face, his anger growing as his expression hardened. He jolted forward, reaching out for the gun.

I pulled the trigger. The bang was so loud as the soldier flew back to the wall with a hole in his shoulder. I couldn't stop staring as he slipped down the wall with his mouth hanging wide in disbelief. His hand went to the wound as Tommy stepped from view.

Bright red blood seeped through the soldier's fingers as the colour once again drained from his face.

"Shit," I said under my breath, looking at Tommy

who just nodded as if he'd agreed with what I'd just done, not caring that I'd shot a man.

"We have to go," his small voice said. And he was right. We had to go because of the sound I'd just made. We had to go because if they found us, we would die. I had to leave this man here alone for his friends to find him so they could bandage him up and stop him from dying. They'd soon expect him back and come in search.

We had to go. We had to go straight away.

I turned, looking to the car, and took a step down the hallway, edging forward, pain reminding me of the slice through the sole of my foot. Glancing back to the soldier gritting his teeth, for a moment I stared at the blood on his hand and the darkening patch of his clothes. My injuries were nothing.

Pleased to be out of his view and down the hall, I heard his gulps of fast breath as I edged closer to the opening and the busy sounds around the village. A distant shout here, a scream there. Engines roaring. Gunfire cracked in the wind with explosions as they searched more houses.

Holding my hand out for Tommy to stay back, I came to the doorway and poked my head out just enough to see down the empty road to the left.

There were no soldiers. No small tanks lumbering around.

I pulled back in, taking a deep breath, then peered around the frame to the right. The soldiers were five houses down already, hammering the door with two large swings and they were in. A loud bang came before the echo died.

It was time.

I pushed the top button on the remote and the lights flashed once as the locks clicked.

"Now," I said without looking back and rushed around to the passenger door, twisting my head left and right as I pulled at the handle. But it was locked and I realised I hadn't checked to see if the key was damaged.

Pressing the button a second time, the locks clicked again and the door pulled open as I grabbed at the handle.

Tommy rushed around me, jumping in the car.

"Stay down," I whispered, as I eased the door closed and ran around the front, taking the driver's seat, then pushed myself as low as I could before I took a moment to catch my breath.

After placing the pistol in the centre console, I looked at Tommy, who'd squeezed into the footwell. He peered up, wide-eyed and hopeful.

I nodded as my breath slowed, looking to the keys in my hand, then to the ignition and the array of controls. I swallowed hard.

I shook my head. I had no time to think of what I could do next. Instead, I moved up in my seat, just a little, and thought back to my mum driving.

There were two pedals, not three. One large one in the middle and one to the right. There was no gear stick, but a selector lever sitting between the two seats along with the handbrake. My breathing became easier as I realised it was an automatic.

Leaning around the steering wheel, I found the key slot and the thin metal slid in with great ease, lighting up the dashboard and telling me to push my foot on the brake before I started the engine.

A smile formed as I realised how helpful the car was being.

I pressed my right foot to the brake.

About to turn the key, I looked to the left and the

muffled voices a little way down the houses. Two soldiers jogged our way. I could guess the anger underneath their gas masks.

"Shit, they've found us."

13

Turning the key, I watched as the soldier's heads snapped up to look our way and I realised although they'd been running towards us, they hadn't been looking at the car. I peered back, no longer in any doubt they'd seen the terror on my face.

Whilst I regretted the decision not to stay hidden until they were inside, looking for the one I'd shot, their rifles rose and I pushed my foot to the right pedal, gritting my teeth through the pain. The engine roared, but we didn't move. Looking to the gear selector, I grabbed it with my left hand through the cloth and pushed down the button on the side as I tensed with the pain in my palm.

Pushing the lever forward, the car groaned with a terrible voice of effort under the bonnet and as I realised I'd left the handbrake up, it released, Tommy lifting out of the footwell and pushing the button on the end of the other lever.

We surged backward. I twisted the wheel left before stomping hard on the brake to stop us in the middle of the road.

Tommy grabbed the selector and slid it into Drive as I jabbed my foot down as hard as I could to the accelerator. We were off.

As I gripped the wheel tight with my good hand, I corrected our direction down the road, only looking in the mirror as the rear windscreen shattered, showering us with glass.

Ducking down as far as I dared, we sped, whilst I held the wheel as straight as I could.

With another shot, I peered ahead, leaning forward in hope of seeing what waited around the corner.

The car stayed on four tyres as I twisted the wheel, the rubber squealing into the turn, seeming as if we would go on two wheels and flip over.

We were about to come out to the road splitting the village in two; the road where at each end there was a roadblock manned by a load of soldiers in gas masks and holding guns they wouldn't hesitate to shoot us with as soon as they saw us.

I slammed on the brakes and we lurched forward, Tommy falling into the footwell, but he climbed back to the seat as we stopped.

"Stay down," I snapped.

Looking around, I cursed having driven in the wrong direction and away from where I was trying to get us to. Knowing we'd be killed straight away if I turned us around and took the quickest route, I couldn't decide if I should loop around the village and come around from the other side or try for somewhere on the opposite side of the village.

The soldiers knew about us now. They knew we had a car and I didn't doubt they'd chase after us. But I couldn't remember if on the other side of the village there was a gap wide enough for us to get through.

What other choice was there? I would just have to go for it. I had to take the chance. I had to build up as much speed as possible as we headed to where we could rush through the fence.

Pushing back down on the accelerator, the pedal

feeling sticky with my blood, I aimed the wheels to take the next corner wide in hope I could keep us on the road at the speed we'd already got to; in hope we'd be out of sight of the soldiers before they reacted.

Our speed grew quickly and I took the turn with the road opening up both sides. I glanced to the left and where the roadblock had been, seeing soldiers standing around, then double taking our way and bringing their guns up to aim.

I looked right and the direction we were turning, but instead of the empty road ahead, the small tank I'd seen before waited in the middle of the tarmac with its thin cannon pointing right at us.

With no idea why they hadn't blown us away already, we raced towards it, unable to stop staring into the barrel. I had no idea why it hadn't moved and didn't adjust its aim when I jolted us to the right, surging out of the sights, only just able to pull us back straight again one-handed.

A gunshot came from behind, but just one. We must have been out of their range. My plan had worked, but as the tyres hit the curb, jumping us on to the path, I fought with the wheel to keep control. Cursing my wounds, the movement forced me to battle the steering with both hands.

We were soon parallel with the small tank. Passing, I glanced to the open back doors and two soldiers with unmasked faces, unloading green metal boxes from the rear.

The soldiers saw us as I saw them, but we passed before they could do anything.

Instead, I watched them in the rear-view mirror, rushing their masks on before shrugging their rifles from their shoulders.

They didn't pull the triggers before we were too far down the road; before I had to make a choice. To go to the left where I didn't know what was happening, or to the right and my house, then around to where I'd planned to break through the fence to reach the woods, but where I knew the soldiers were looking for me, ready to pull their triggers.

I chose to stick to the plan. I chose to head to the right. It was the only way I knew would take us to the woods and the promise of safety if we weren't going to navigate over the fields in a vain hope the car could cope with the ruts of churned mud.

Seeing the roadblock ahead and the soldiers readying their aims but not firing, I caught sight of another group to the left, but they weren't soldiers. These were people in bright orange space-like suits, with pipes snaking across the outside. They stood in groups of three or more, looking down to rows of long black body bags lying in lines across the ground.

My breath caught in my throat and I looked away, blinking as if that would erase the image. Then I saw the corner and slowed a little, reminded of the pain when we'd last hit the curb.

As the turn opened out, I looked ahead, expecting the soldiers to be where we'd left them. I was in no doubt they were expecting us to come around and had their guns ready to meet us.

I slowed right down before we'd completed the turn, uncertain of whether I should race ahead or creep around the corner in case I needed to make a different move and head back the way we'd come. But I didn't complete the thought before Tommy called out.

"Mum," he shouted, the word long and drawn out.

Before I could look to see who he called to and

just as I realised what he'd said, his door opened. I slammed on the brakes, tensing with the pain as Tommy jumped to the road, running with his arms open toward his mum emerging from a walkway between two houses.

I stared with relief that there was an adult who could take charge, a mother, someone who would look after us. Someone who would know what to do.

With no time to relax as Tommy ran, I took in the detail of what I'd seen. Rising in my seat, I pulled the door open to get a better look and make sure I'd seen right and that the woman about to grip around Tommy wasn't really missing the side of her face.

As I looked on I realised the sight hadn't been a figment of my imagination. The white of her skull where the skin down one side of her face should have been. The red of blood dripping down around the edges. She ambled along, opening her arms to the boy so close to her.

Despite all I'd seen, people's behaviour was so much like those in my favourite video game; I couldn't bring myself to believe the explanation. But I realised enough to know it wasn't right. I thought back to the body bags and for the first time thought perhaps the soldiers had the best idea.

After ducking back into the car, I pulled the pistol from the centre console. I attempted to run, despite the pain in my right foot, towards the woman.

I was too late. She had Tommy in her arms and rather than pulling him close in an embrace and a beautiful reunion, she gripped him around his torso and sunk her teeth into the sleeve of his hoodie.

14

Tommy screamed, trying to pull back, but it looked as if her grip was too strong for his effort to make an impact. I tried to hurry toward him, pushing the gun out in front but I wasn't stupid enough to think I had any chance of hitting her from even this short distance. I would most likely miss, but had an equal chance of hitting Tommy.

I rushed forward as best as I could and called out to him to pull away. I saw his effort, but her grip was too tight as she tried to pull him closer to take another bite.

He struggled as I grew nearer with the gun still out in front, but it was only when I was within two arm lengths that I dared to fire, the bullet smashing into her eye socket. I shot again, missing this time, the round pinging off the brickwork at her back.

The first had been enough and she released her grip, falling to the floor.

"Get in the car," I shouted, still looking at the woman who wasn't Tommy's mum anymore.

With his hand at where she'd bitten his arm, Tommy looked to me wide-eyed, nodding at the instruction as he rushed to the open door. With skin so pale and his jaw hanging slack, he'd been so lucky he was wearing the hoodie; otherwise she'd have broken the skin and it would be two of us with wounds we'd somehow have to deal with.

On my way around the front of the car, I had to stop, resting on the bonnet for a moment's respite from the pain in my foot. Looking down, I took solace it wasn't pouring with blood.

I knew if Mum could see me she would have a fit at how dirty it was and make me bathe in antiseptic.

But she would never be there for me again. And neither would Tommy's for him. We were alone.

A gunshot echoing in the distance pulled me back

from my spiralling mood and to the road and the corner we had to go around before we were out of this place. But we had to be quick. If the soldiers weren't already rushing after us, then the gunshots would soon bring them near.

Gritting my teeth, I put one foot after the other, feeling the pain rising once again. I made it around the car soon enough, landing down in the seat.

Glancing to Tommy, he still held his hand to his arm. "Are you okay?" I said. "Silly question, I know." But rather than bursting into tears, he looked down at my foot and up to the blood-soaked towel in my hand. He gave a slow nod.

Through the missing back window came the sound of a great engine starting, then revving high. My thoughts flashed to the tank and shaking my head, I manhandled the seatbelt, clipping it into place and we were off again into the corner.

With my foot pushing down the accelerator, we passed the car crash outside my house. I paid little attention, knowing I had to pick a speed fast enough for our momentum to carry us through the fence, but slow enough that I could see between the houses; controlled enough not to smash to the brick and bring this nightmare to an end.

I released the throttle just a little. The street was empty.

"Seat belt, Tommy," I said as I glanced to his side, hoping he had enough time to pull it on.

I scanned along the houses, the open doors, searching for the truck and the soldiers and trying to figure out where they had gone. Then I realised they were probably catching up behind us. We had no time to wait.

Shaking away the worry, I searched for the gap

between the houses as I visualised the fence beyond. Then I saw it, the gap I needed, and pushed for more speed.

I took the turn, the tyres squealing as I gritted my teeth, remembering the curb at the edge of the pavement. I looked up as the front wheel crashed against the curb. It felt like the tyres were rock hard, but we were over and somehow they were still attached. The rear wheels hit hard moments after.

Now there was nothing between us and the fence. Concentrating as hard as I could, I lined up to the centre of the tall metal panel, correcting left and then right and left again, whilst looking to the thin gaps on either side and the concrete blocks on the legs.

A sudden thought came to mind; what if there was more concrete on the other side in the middle of the panel to stop anyone breaking through?

But we had no choice; any moment we would hit and we would know for sure.

I glanced again to Tommy sitting in his seat, gripping the sides of the upholstery and gritting his teeth, eyes closed as we raced forward.

A vision flashed in my head that the fence would hold firm and we'd slam right into it, snapping our necks as if we'd hit a brick wall. But it was too late. Nothing could change that now.

The impact came with a great bang, but then was gone.

We'd hit the fence, pinning us into our seats, but we kept on moving. My worst fears hadn't come true and as the bass sound of the crash and its echo slowly faded, I saw the woods ahead, the view rising and falling as the car jumped up and down in the ruts.

Steam or smoke, I wasn't sure which, sprayed out

from the front of the car and I pushed the brake, afraid of the engine exploding and taking us with it.

"Get out," I shouted, glancing at Tommy to make sure he was okay.

He stared at the white billowing vapour. We pulled at the door handles at the same time and I regretted jumping to the grass.

As the pain in my foot subsided, I looked back to where we'd come and the concrete blocks still in place. The metal panel lay to the side, its once straight lines all buckled and bent. I thought for a moment about lifting it up and leaning it back in place to give us the slimmest of chances of pretending we hadn't just done what we had. But even if I could carry such a weight, I had no chance with only one of my hands unhurt.

I turned, rushing as fast as I could past the car, Tommy already at the tree line. I caught him up and we ran, the feeling so great to be outside of the fence with only the trees on either side.

Despite the pain the forest floor caused to my foot, the dirt clogged my slipper as I walked, matting with my blood to form a kind of protective sole.

We slowed after a few minutes, both of us turning the way we'd come. Relief rushed over me when I couldn't see the village, or the fence, or the rising smoke, for the canopy.

We'd made it. We'd stayed alive. I'd rescued Tommy and now we could hear the main road just up ahead, even if we couldn't see it yet.

I looked down to Tommy, not able to drop my smile. He looked up, seeming so pale in the forest light.

"It'll be okay," I said. I spotted his hand hovering where his mother had bitten him, for the first time seeing the dried blood between his fingers.

As he pulled his hand away I saw the tear in the fabric and what looked like a wound underneath.

"I don't feel very well," he said in a soft voice.

"It's okay. A few minutes more and we'll get you some help. It will all be fine," I said.

But little did I know.

Discover the fate of humanity by searching 'In The End' on Amazon or check out **www.gjstevens.com** for signed copies.

Printed in Great Britain
by Amazon